AFTER THE HAZE

AFTER THE HAZE

JACQUELINE DRUGA

Published by Vulpine Press in the United Kingdom in 2023

Cover photo by Dallas Clemmens

ISBN: 978-1-83919-503-7

www.vulpine-press.com

To Caroline Jane Rochey for the incredible help and support
you have given me with my books

Also by Jacqueline Druga:

Empty Earth
Into the Ash
My Dead World
No Man's Land
Omnicide
Static
The Following
The Last Woman
The Spread
Three Days to Impact
What we Become
Winter Burn

ONE

WHERE ART THOU?

Gideon Falls Community, Missouri

"Mom, Vincent's gone."

Avery entered the cabin, making the statement so nonchalantly; I didn't pay much attention. At fifteen years old, she wasn't whiney or full of drama like a lot of girls that age. She merely walked in and set the basket of laundry on the couch in the living room.

I removed the pot from the wood burning stove, put it on the kitchen table, and glanced over at her.

"Oh, thank you for getting that off the line. Does it smell okay? I tried some new—"

"Mom, did you not hear what I said? Vincent is gone."

"What do you mean gone?"

"He left," she replied.

"Maybe he went to Mr. Parson's. He is always there."

"No, Mom, I saw him. A couple hours ago he said goodbye, I thought he went there, too, but I just saw Macy, and she said she saw Vincent heading down the road with a huge backpack."

"You didn't see a backpack when he said goodbye?"

Avery shook her head.

"Then he went to Parson's or fishing with that boy." I waved my hand. "You know the one he finds annoying." Turning, I went back toward the stove.

"Can we check his room?" Avery said. "I have a bad feeling."

"Sweetie, where would he go? Why would he go?" I stared at her. Then I saw it. She was truly concerned as if she knew more than she was telling. "Fine. Let's check."

Vincent being 'gone' was just inconceivable to me.

We were happy, we really were. Life was perfect there. Gideon Falls. A small hidden community located in the woods, near a lake on the border of Kentucky and Missouri, south of St. Louis.

A community of twenty-five, all living in cabins, off the land.

No electricity, no phones, no outside influence. No news to dampen your day or consume your every emotion.

When we moved there a few months earlier, it was just what we needed as a family, and it worked for us so we stayed. My father-in-law, Morris, stayed for a week then visited often. No one, not Vincent, not Avery, *no one* complained.

So, I didn't worry about Vincent being gone.

We had just settled in, harvested our first garden, were getting in the swing of things. Vincent even made a friend.

Just the night before we played trivia to all hours. Vincent gave no indication that he hated it or wanted to leave.

Vincent wasn't gone.

To me, there was a chance he went with Mr. Parson's nephew into town to get supplies. He had been saying he wanted to do that. Maybe Avery just misunderstood.

However, the moment I climbed the stairs to his bedroom loft above the living room, I knew in a simple glance my daughter wasn't exaggerating.

Pictures were gone, the ones on his dresser of the family, along with those old trading cards he had on his nightstand.

My heart sunk.

Why wouldn't he say anything? Why would he just go?

Something wasn't right.

It was time to search for my son, and not for the first time in my life. Though this time was different. The last time I searched, it wasn't just for my son, it was for my entire family.

TWO

TUMBLING DOWN

Four Months Earlier
Steubenville, OH

It was warm and something about it was bitter as it crossed against my lips, seeping into my mouth. The taste of it woke me, brought me to consciousness and then all of my other senses kicked in as I slowly became aware. A brain fog still clouded my clear thinking, making it unable for me to register what had happened.

My eyes were open, but it was dark, I couldn't see anything. I was on my back, slanted headfirst upward. I could feel bricks or wood under me and in the distance, dripping water, cries, moans and screams.

My head hurt, but nowhere specific that I could feel. I didn't feel injured. I wiggled my fingers, toes, and shifted my legs and arms.

After I knew I wasn't hurt, I extended my arm reaching up into the darkness. It took quite a reach to touch something. I wasn't crammed in some dark space.

That was a good thing.

I rolled to my side and reached into my back pocket there. I didn't bring a purse with me, so that was where I kept my phone.

Praying and hoping it wasn't busted, I lifted it. It illuminated. The screen was cracked, I had half my battery and no signal.

I bit my bottom lip as I put on the phone's flashlight. The taste was there still.

At first, I thought it had to be blood. Reaching up with my fingers, I felt the moistness and when I brought them under the light, I saw it was black.

Oil or something.

Those first few moments of coming to consciousness were like waking up after a deep sleep and forgetting you had to be somewhere.

Suddenly, I was struck with an intense wave of panic.

Oh my God. My family.

"Vincent!" I called my son's name, then followed with a cry for my daughter and husband. "Avery! Ted!"

Nothing.

"Vincent! Avery! Ted!" I screamed my loudest.

"Mom!"

My daughter's voice. She sounded scared, weak, far away.

"Avery!"

"Mommy, help me!"

I could hear the sobbing in her voice. I panicked even more.

"Baby, I'm coming. I'll find you. Call my name. Keep calling my name."

She did and I turned to find the direction her voice came from.

She couldn't be that far; we were all together, the four of us, when it happened.

Avery called my name, intermittently sobbing. I thought I locked on to where it came from, but others started calling out for help, drowning out the sound of my daughter's voice.

I wanted to scream to tell them to shut up.

Just shut up!

I knew they had to be scared, but they didn't start screaming out like that until Avery and I vocally connected.

"Avery!" I called her. "Vincent."

"Someone help us," a voice cried out.

"Lady, can you hear me? I'm here. Call for help."

"Anyone there?"

"My legs are crushed. Help!"

All those people calling out, making it so hard for me to hear if my own flesh and blood was still there, still calling.

It was maddening.

Reeling in desperation and anger, I crawled my way to the sound. I couldn't see any light; it was just black. If nothing else, I was determined.

I would find my family.

THREE

THE TOUR

How did we get there?

We were standing on that third level walkway, listening to the historian and tour guide, telling us about men who worked there back in the day.

"Those men made history," the guide said. *"They built this country and now all of you are here to witness a new era in this city."*

I distinctly remembered him saying that line, only because there was tall pregnant girl who raced out of the tour, brushing by me, hand over her mouth. She looked pale. I felt bad for her. It was pretty warm in there that was probably what made her sick. The tour guide didn't miss a beat. Like a robot, he kept going. I suppose he was well rehearsed. This was his big moment.

Admittedly, for the longest time, I didn't get it.

Ted talked about it for two years before the project got off the ground.

I listened but thought he was a little overzealous, but it turned out, I was wrong.

He had every right to be excited; the news, magazines, they covered it like crazy.

The old, run-down steel mill, situated on the riverbank in Steubenville, Ohio, was being transformed to a plant where they converted materials to be used to create biomass energy.

The first of its kind on that grand of a scale. A safe, natural, heating and electricity alternative.

Anything waste plant based, either from industry, home or farms could be converted. The river ways offered ease of transportation to get the materials to and from the Bio Plant.

All in little Steubenville, Ohio. A city that once was a relic of the past, was to be a posterchild for the future.

The entire project was seven years in the making.

Vincent had just started fifth grade when Ted began talking about it. Now Vincent was about to go into his senior year. Avery, a sophomore. Both our kids spent most of their lives, first listening to Ted, then waving goodbye every Sunday when he left to work the week as a construction superintendent at the site, the old steel mill, a thousand miles from home.

He commuted as often as he could.

I often joked that was what made our marriage so strong.

When people would ask, "Lucy, what is the secret?"

I would tell them, "I never see my husband."

When it was finished and the official christening day was upon us, we joined Ted.

He was so proud.

Ted wasn't a big wig, he was just a construction super, yet my dashing husband stood like a peacock with his chest out that day, watching as his bosses and the vice president of the United States cut the ribbon.

It was a monumental event, and we as a family were privileged to be there.

I was glad the kids came along. We did give them the opportunity to stay back with Ted's father; being that it was just the start of summer, typically all they wanted to do was nothing but sleep, but, to our surprise, they wanted to come.

They were pretty excited as we lined up for the tour, I don't think it was the presence of the vice president and other politicians, or the green construction hard hats everyone got to wear. It was that Sonya Haze, actress turned humanitarian or something or other, was there.

She was sporting the hardhat in all her glam looking absolutely beautiful.

It was a media circus out front. Only a few reporters were able to go in. A part of me didn't understand the frenzy, even the vice president was using it as part of his election platform.

One hundred and fifty people, including families of workers, celebrities and politicians, began to go inside.

Little did I know, all one hundred and fifty people would soon be trapped.

There were three tours going on at the same time. Celebrity Sonya ended up on our tour and Vincent was hyper about it. He tried to act 'cool,' but he kept inching his way farther from us and nearer to the front by her, hoping to get a picture.

I kept telling him he'd get a chance at the luncheon. But, no, he kept moving forward.

Ted and I laughed about it because it was so unlike Vincent. He cared what people thought about him, embarrassed easily, and hated authority.

Avery was even more a surprise; she was into the alternate energy. She asked a lot of questions, often lagging few feet behind the group, taking in the sights.

When it happened, three people were between Vince and us. I was next to Ted, and Avery was an arm's length away. I had just reached to her to move her along when the four loud booms erupted from somewhere in the structure.

They were deafening, causing my ears to ring.

The entire platform shook as if hit by an earthquake. It was just a few seconds, that was it.

Enough time for me to fearfully look at Ted, and call out his name.

Then everything just…tumbled.

I did as well.

It all went black.

FOUR

THE DARK

"Mommy, help!"

She did it. Avery broke through. She waited for a second of opportunity and she used her strength to call my name.

I was headed in the right direction; I was certain where her voice was coming from.

Despite hearing my daughter, I didn't stop screaming for Vincent or Ted. Calling out their names every inch that I crawled.

It didn't seem as if anyone was around me.

I tried to figure out where I was in the collapsed building, how did I end up so far from everyone?

It was definitely some sort of explosion. It brought the entire building down. At least the huge part we were in. I could smell a hint of burning, but I wasn't choking on smoke.

Where some people would think accident, I immediately went to war.

For seven years, from plotting, planning, building to finish, the wonder plant of the future was in the works. Surely, in the event of war, Steubenville had gone from an inconsequential city to a prime target.

It wasn't anywhere inconceivable that we were now at war.

What if we had been hit with a nuclear weapon?

Like most people I went extreme. Worst-case scenario. News of an epidemic was always the 'big one' to me and I ran to buy toilet paper and supplies. Not because I was this big prepper. Heck, I never bothered to learn much. I just did what everyone else was doing. If they were stocking up on toilet paper and ramen, then damn it, so was I.

I was not a leader; I was a follower and that was something Ted got irritated with me about.

"Lucy, if you want to act like the big survivalist, you really should learn more," he'd say. "So, learn or we don't renew the Sam's Club card."

So, I sort of learned about nuclear war. Sort of. I knew it came with radiation.

As I crawled toward the voices, I started growing fearful of radiation.

How would we survive it? We were far from home, far from anything. We'd be like those people in the movies, or in books, on the road trying to make it somewhere. Because according to books and movies, every survival story is a road trip.

I was buried in my thoughts as much as I was buried in rubble.

I had to stop thinking about the 'what ifs' and focus on finding my family.

One thing at a time.

Find my family, figure a way out, then worry about what to do next.

In my mind it was a global or at the very least, national, catastrophe and no one was coming to help.

Phone in hand with the light leading the way, I followed the sounds of the voices. My hands feeling the uneven ground beneath my hands and knees. Concrete, metal, bricks, that was what it felt like. Each inch, drawing closer to the crying voices.

I saw an opening ahead; it was slightly lighter than where I was. Either someone had a flashlight or there was an external light source.

Getting close to that filled me with enthusiasm and I picked up the pace until my hand sunk through the rubble and landed on something soft.

I knew by the feel beneath my fingers it was a person. A sickening feeling filled my gut and shaking, I brought the flashlight up to see.

Scared to death that it was my husband or son, I shone the light down.

The beam of my phone's light reflected off of the gray pupil of the dead man's eyes.

His face was bloody, nose smashed, but I exhaled in relief because it wasn't Ted or Vincent.

I moved onward, calling out my family's names. Others replied and their voices were louder.

There was a triangular shaped opening and I crawled through, as soon as I did it was open and bigger. High above, a hundred feet at least, the sun poked through a huge hole in the ceiling.

Around me was not only debris, but bodies.

There were so many people. Some moved, some didn't.

"Avery!" I called out.

"Mom. Mom! Mom, over here."

She was close, I could tell, and she was to my right. I turned my body and scurried, following the sound of her voice.

As painful as it was, I ignored the other calls for help. People reaching for me, grabbing me. I just wanted to tell them I would be back, but I had to get to my child first.

It was light enough in there that I didn't need my flashlight, but I was glad I did.

Just as I was about to shut it off to conserve power, I not only noticed that I had a signal, but the beam caught my daughter's face.

I found her.

All I saw was her head, resting on a pillow of debris. She was covered almost completely by the body of a woman.

"Baby, I'm here." I rushed to her, laying my hand on her face.

"Mommy, I can't breathe," she said. "She's crushing me."

"I'll get you."

"Where's Dad? Vincent?" Avery asked.

"I don't know."

"What happened?"

"I don't know. Just stay still. Does anything hurt?"

"Just my chest. I can't breathe."

I assumed the woman was dead, but when I reached for her, the woman screamed horridly.

A painfully loud wail.

"No!" the woman cried. "Don't touch me. Don't. My neck. I think it's gonna break. Don't touch me. It'll break. I feel it." The woman tensed up and Avery cried.

"Mommy." Avery sobbed. "I can't…I can't…breathe."

My child, my beautiful child. I couldn't tell if she was hurt or how badly. Maybe if I moved the woman just a bit, it would help.

Again, I reached for the woman, that's when I noticed, debris had fallen on her. I lifted the piece of concrete from the woman's gut. It didn't bring her relief, it only caused more screaming.

And Avery, she coughed. She sounded as if she were choking.

"Mom," her words weakly croaked out.

As cold as it seemed I had to make a decision and I chose my daughter.

I gripped the shoulder of the woman laying across her. "I'm sorry," I said. "I have to help my daughter."

"No. No. No. Please," the woman begged.

"I'm sorry."

"No."

I only lifted her a foot and…crack.

I heard it.

It sounded like a twig breaking, but I knew when the woman went instantly lifeless that it wasn't a twig, it was her neck.

My whole body tensed up in an immediate cringe and I moved the woman as fast as I could, shuddering and shaking for a second before I grabbed onto Avery.

My daughter clutched me.

"Are you hurt?" I asked. "Anything."

Avery shook her head, sobbing.

"It's okay. You're okay," I said. "We're gonna find Vincent and Dad and we're getting out of here. I'll figure it out."

And I saw my phone in my hand.

The signal was weak, but it was there.

I pulled back from holding my daughter and lifted my phone. I didn't know if there was even help out there, but I had the means in my hand to find out.

In that moment, Avery's head resting against my chest, I called for help.

FIVE

THE HOLE GROWS DARK

The call went through. My heart relaxed and I breathed out. Immediately a wave of nervousness overtook me and I trembled.

"911, what is your emergency?"

"We're trapped. Please send someone to help us," I said. "We were visiting a plant, I don't know the street, we're from out of town."

"Ma'am, are you from the West Tech Biomass Energy plant?"

"Yes."

"We are aware of the situation and help is on the way. What is your name?" she asked.

"Lucy Carver."

"Lucy, are you injured?"

"No. I don't think, my daughter is."

"Is she breathing?" she asked.

"Yes, she is conscious, but was under things, people. I don't know if anything's broken. I can't find my son or husband."

"Ma'am, help is on the way," she said. "Do you remember where you were when the explosion happened?"

"We were on a tour, not sure where in the plant."

"That's fine."

"There's a hole. There's a hole in the roof above me, I can see the sky. It's bright. It's high though."

"How many injured are there?" she asked. "Anyone else around you injured?"

I was about to answer her, and I froze when my eyes cast down to the woman I'd moved to save my daughter. The same woman who'd died because I moved her. She lay on her side as if I tossed her aside.

In a way I did. At the moment I moved her, I thought only about saving my daughter. I didn't think moving her would cause her neck to snap.

But it did.

It was something I would have to live with. Staring at her, immediately I was hit with guilt. Guilt I didn't feel when it happened.

"Ma'am. Mrs. Carver," the 911 operator called for me. "Ma'am, are you still there?"

"Yes. Yes, I am. I'm sorry. There are injured. I don't know how badly. There are a lot of dead."

"Ma'am, could you do me a favor and not make any more calls. I need you to leave the phone on and just set it somewhere. We're going to use it to track you."

"Thank you."

"Please know help is there now. According to my screen they just arrived."

"What happened?" I asked.

"I can't confirm, but it was an attack."

"Nuclear?" I asked, immediately feeling stupid for asking that. Of course, it wasn't a nuclear attack, I reached emergency services.

"No, ma'am, we are receiving reports it was a deliberate attack. Now I am going to stay connected, if you need me, call out. But keep the phone line clear."

"I will thank you."

I lowered the phone and cradled my daughter, kissing her on the top of her head. "Help's on the way."

"I'm scared," my daughter wept.

"Me, too."

An attack. A deliberate one. The only thing that I could think of that would hit with such magnitude was a terrorist attack.

All the media, cameras outside, the celebrities and vice president. It was primed and ready for a terror attack. Despite all the security, somehow, they hit the plant.

Who was it? Why do it?

Twenty minutes after initially placing the call, my phone buzzed and beeped. It wasn't a call or message, it was the tracking.

An hour later, a voice from above called down.

"Steubenville Fire and Rescue, anyone there."

I didn't have to say anything, people cried out and screamed.

"We're coming down," he said. "Stay where you are."

What the firefighter and EMS worker didn't realize was not many could move. They were trapped.

I peered up to that hole in the ceiling and saw two emergency workers slowly descending. They were in one of those open-topped, small, squared carriages, like a small elevator.

They were being lowered by a line and I could see it was connected to some sort of crane.

When they arrived in our area, people vied for their attention, calling out and screaming for help.

I didn't know much about search and rescue, but by the way they acted, they were there to assess.

The entire structure had imploded in a way, and by some miracle, created a cave of destruction beneath the hole. Digging people out was impossible because the whole thing was like a Jenga game, one wrong move and it all would fall.

The only way to get us out was one or two at a time by that carriage.

Avery and I watched as they approached different people, then my phone did that tracking noise again.

Within seconds, the one firefighter came over to me, following the sound.

"Mrs. Carver," he said.

"Yes, that's me."

"Are you hurt?"

"No but my daughter is. I don't think she's hurt too badly and I don't think anything is broken."

He crouched down to Avery, shining a flashlight in her eyes. He then examined her head. Feeling it. "What's your name?" he asked her.

"Avery."

"Avery does anything hurt?"

"My head. My chest where that lady fell on it."

"Arms and legs?" he questioned.

"Fine."

"Good." He pulled from his coat pocket a small bottle of water and handed it to her. "Drink this. We'll get you out of here." He then looked at me. "Mrs. Carver, I promise you we will safely get everyone out. But we need to get the critically injured out first. So hang tight, it might be a while, but we'll get you out."

"Can I look for my husband and son?"

"We'll find them," he said assuredly. "We'll find everyone."

When he walked away, I knew it was going to be a *long* while. There was no way they could fit more than four people in that carriage, and if one was severely injured that was all that took.

They loaded the injured on slowly and it rose at a snail's pace.

I resigned myself to the fact that Avery and I were a long way down the waiting list.

But I watched. I watched every single person they loaded in that carriage, looking for my husband and son.

It took three hours for them to get Avery, leaving me behind. I was fine, other than the dead, I would be one of the last taken out.

It grew dark fast, and they aimed a spotlight over the opening. It didn't help much. I swore I was one of the last people remaining.

I sat in the dark for the longest time, straining to see who they pulled out. My daughter was safe, I took comfort in that. But my husband and son were still lost. At least from what I knew.

There was a chance that they were out. They didn't get hurt.

I held on to that hope.

Somehow they narrowly escaped, that had to be the explanation. I scanned the rubble with the flashlight of my phone until my battery died.

I didn't find them or see them.

They were somewhere and I prayed they weren't one of the dead.

Finally, it was my turn. By the time they got me, I was cold, hungry and tired.

They placed a blanket over my shoulders as they loaded me on the carriage, me and another man. He was in a state of shock, like me.

One rescue worker accompanied us as we lifted slowly.

As we rose above the wreckage, the spotlight illuminated the devastation done to the magnificent building.

It was splinters and pieces.

Like an amusement park ride, the crane swung away from the rubble and lowered us to the awaiting ambulances.

The second we touched down, cameras flashed, reporters shouted questions.

Were they insane? Did they not see what we had gone through? Did they seriously think I was going to answer a question on whether we were scared?

Of course, we were. Who wouldn't be?

Once safely on the ground, they rushed us to an ambulance, and we were loaded inside.

I tried looking over my shoulder, to see if there was anyone else. But they moved us so fast I couldn't.

The doors to the ambulance closed.

It was done for me. I was out, I was freed, but I wasn't at ease.

Because I still didn't know the whereabouts of my family.

SIX

GUILT ROUND TWO

When a tragic event unfolds, a disaster, and you're not a part of it, it is a totally different beast.

An armchair spectator with a front seat to everything that happens. Every news story, picture, and social media post.

All there, but when you're on the inside it is not the same.

Having worked for years in the costume department at the local theater, I knew firsthand that what the audience saw was not what went on behind the scenes.

The horrendous event at the Biomass plant was no different for the person watching at home or on their phone, than the theater-goer sat in the audience.

They couldn't feel the blood sweat and tears. Absolutely, the show would move them, but not like those that were a part of it.

I didn't cry after I was rescued. I wanted to, I felt it in my chest, but I was in such a state of shock, I couldn't even think correctly.

How did I survive with barely a scratch?

To make matters worse, they took me to a hotel, where I was placed in a banquet hall. A few EMS workers handing out bandages, coffee and food. Families reunited with those few who weren't injured badly enough to warrant a hospital stay. While others waited for news of loved ones.

I was in the wrong place. I wasn't a family member that had seen the news and come rushing to collect their loved one, and I wasn't injured waiting for my family to take me home.

I needed to *find* my family.

My son and husband were nowhere to be found and I knew Avery wasn't going to be in the hotel either.

Every time I tried to talk to someone, I was moved to another person.

"Oh, try that woman over there in the blue sweater," directed someone.

Blue sweater woman told me to see the man in green. That man sent me elsewhere in the big giant room.

People crying in joy, hugging loved ones. Reporters being ejected from the private reunions. All the while, anyone who passed me tried to offer aid, noticing I was a survivor, meandering around in a zombie state with dirty clothes, a brush burned forehead and oil smeared on my lips.

I didn't need help. I needed my family.

Here, have a coffee.

Are you hungry?

Maybe you should sit down.

Stop.

STOP!

Standing center of the room, my inner anger and anguish, released in the form of a scream that I didn't even realize had from me until everyone drew silent and began to stare.

Shoulders moving heavily up and down, as I wheezed out a few breaths and said simply, "I want my family."

Jules Montgomery was his name. And the moment he led me out of the ballroom was the first time I had seen him in the hours I'd spent at the hotel. I would have noticed him. He looked like a weatherman having a bad day. A middle-aged man in a suit and tie, an outfit that looked as if he had been wearing it all day. Not quite as crisp as it probably was when he put it on. He saw me in the center of that hall and escorted me out. He was calm about it and I thought maybe he was taking me to an office. Instead, he took me to the hotel bar.

It was empty except for the bartender that dried glasses while watching the television. We sat down at the bar.

"Drink of choice?" Jules asked me.

"I just want to find answers."

"And I am here to give you what I can," Jules said.

"I don't think being in this hotel can give me my answers."

"This is the best place you can be. Now, drink of choice."

"Bourbon, straight."

Jules signaled the bartender with two fingers. "Two waters, two bourbons neat. And could you shut that off." He indicated to the television. "Please. Thank you."

My eyes lifted to the television and briefly saw the words, 'Terror in America,' before the set was shut down.

"You don't need to see it. You lived it. You'll keep living it. And it is going to stay with you in more ways than one." He nodded a thanks to the bartender who set down the drinks before this.

"Jules, I feel anxious. I need to be out there looking for my family."

"I know. Trust me we are more organized than you think. I can't keep track of those few that survived if you guys are out there looking through the rubble, or finding a hospital. And let's not forget the reporters out there. They're looking for you."

"It was a terror attack?" I sipped my drink. It did feel good, the warmth of it rolling down my chest. I needed it to calm me.

Jules nodded. "We don't know who or why. Not yet. We may never, but there are probably going to be more. That's the intel I have."

"And your job?" I asked.

"I am an information liaison for the Department of Emergency Management. I get information and relay it. I haven't stopped since we started the rescue. I have been reuniting the injured or news of them with their families in there."

I brought my glass to my mouth and sipped again. "News of the dead?"

"That, too. Those that we can identify. There are still quite a few we haven't yet."

"That many."

"It's horrific. Two hundred and twelve people, guests and workers were there. Only four escaped without anything, you're one. We estimate about a hundred and fifty dead. We're hopeful we can still find survivors in the rubble, though it's not likely."

I shifted my eyes to him, swallowing the lump in my throat. "You said you are here to give me the answers that you can."

Jules nodded. "I didn't just grab you because of the outburst. I came for you. If you were out there, I wouldn't be able to find you and tell you that your son, Vincent Carver is alive and only broke his hand."

I wheezed out in relief nearly toppling my glass. I caught it.

"Your daughter is fine, a couple bumps and bruises. Both will be brought here in the next hour or two. They're with counselors now."

"And my husband?"

"I'm sorry. Ted didn't make it."

I felt a wave of sickness hit me. "Are you sure?"

"Vincent was the one that told us. He found him."

I didn't know how to react. I just didn't. It wasn't real. It didn't seem it. I wanted to break down and cry. Throw myself on the floor in a massive sobbing fit, but the tears wouldn't come. The only thing I could do at that moment was close my eyes tightly, bring the drink to my lips and absorb the news I was just given.

I was torn between overwhelming looming grief over the loss of my life partner and joy that my children survived a tragedy.

It was the start of our story.

The beginning of a fear that stayed with me. I didn't see the entire Biomass terror attack as a preparation, it was punch in the gut. I wasn't ready for the changes that were before me and I needed to be in control. But everything laid the groundwork for the unconventional decision I would make for me and my children.

Decisions that would once again save our lives, I just didn't know it that fateful night in the hotel bar.

SEVEN

IN SEARCH OF VINCENT AGAIN

Gideon Falls Community, Missouri

Grief was supposed to be personal.

Before the terror attack, we were just a normal family from Missouri. A husband in construction, a wife who worked at the bank as a teller, two teenagers. Couldn't get more typical if we tried.

In a snap of a finger, the explosion of a building, our lives were in the spotlight.

We were three of forty who made it out of that building, and after a few days, with hospital deaths, that number dwindled down to just thirty. We probably would have slipped by unnoticed, like several other of the survivors, had Vincent not been responsible for saving celebrity Sonya Haze. He not only lifted debris from her, he used his shirt to make a tourniquet and didn't wait for a rescue, he found their way out before I had even emerged from the rubble.

He saved her life and she didn't stop talking about it. About how she'd be dead if it wasn't for him. How he put aside his own grief of finding his father's body to help her.

That week before the funeral was insanity. We escaped back to our home outside of St. Louis to wait for Ted's body, but they found us. Reporters parked outside our house, followed us to the store and even the funeral home.

Our phones never stopped ringing, text messages plowed through, and my husband's face was plastered everywhere.

The actual funeral needed security; it was all too much. Everywhere we turned was news of the attack, of Ted, of our loss.

I found myself wishing something else would happen to take the attention off of us.

Sonya apologized for igniting the circus fire. I didn't blame her, she wasn't doing it for attention, she was doing it out of gratefulness. It was innocent. It really was.

But like she attributed Vincent to saving her life, I attributed her to saving mine. I was at the end, I was worried about my children and at the funeral, when I told her I was waiting on the insurance money to escape with my kids, she made it happen.

The next day we were packing. I could have said no, but I needed to go. Get away.

Sonya had her people find the perfect place. People meaning her famous father, Christoph. It wasn't far from our home. Secluded cabin in an off the grid community. No phones, no television, the only power was a solar generator. Of course, our nearest neighbor was Mr. Parson and he was a good twenty-minute walk from our place.

Sonya's father knew Mr. Gideon who started the community. Mr. Gideon had recently passed and his amazing cabin was for sale.

She bought it for us, in our name. It would be ours whenever we needed it.

In our grief it was what we needed.

It offered us the solitude and buzz free world we needed to heal.

Two weeks was the plan, but we never left.

I blame myself for being selfish. I did ask the kids early on if it was okay if we stayed, they didn't voice an opposition.

There were a couple kids their age in the area, Vincent made a friend. Avery didn't want to be bothered.

We were not only healing from the terror attack, but from the loss of Ted.

I loved the simplicity of our new life. I never went back to or even called my job, I just simply disappeared with my family. If we needed supplies, we got a list to Mr. Parson, and his nephew would pick it up on his trip to town.

Avery liked the new life too, at least I believed that. Vincent liked it when he was with us.

He had his secrets.

I knew he slipped away with Jeff, Mr. Parson's nephew. Taking trips to the city, like a junkie, getting his technology fix.

He didn't say anything to me and I said nothing to him. Not like he was doing anything wrong or breaking any laws. It was his thing and as long as he was happy, I was happy.

That was why it surprised me so much when Vincent left.

If he hadn't taken things like pictures and his prize trading cards, I wouldn't have thought he was just doing his thing again.

Avery and I took a walk to Mr. Parson's cabin.

Macy, a girl who often popped by had said she saw Vincent with a large backpack. Mr. Parson confirmed that but said Vincent was headed to Jeff's.

Another half hour of walking Avery and I arrived. Jeff's truck was gone but his wife Linda was there, sitting on the porch.

"Looking for Vincent?" Linda asked.

"Yeah, we are. He said goodbye but had a backpack."

Linda nodded. "They went to town. Supplies."

"So he did go with Jeff?" I asked.

"Yes, he did. They'll be back shortly. I expect them in about an hour."

"Mom," Avery whispered. "Ask her if she knows."

"Knows what?" Linda questioned.

"Vincent had taken his trading cards and some photos. Is there a chance Jeff is dropping him somewhere."

Linda smiled. "Do you think he's running away?"

"I'm afraid of it."

Linda shook her head. "He showed me the pictures. Just tossing this out there. Your birthday is coming up, Lucy. Maybe he's doing something with those pictures and those trading cards are a way to pay for them."

"How would you know all this?" Avery asked suspiciously. "Did he tell you?"

"I just heard him say to Jeff about selling them. And that he didn't want to disappoint your mom on her birthday."

Avery hummed out a 'hmm.'

"Avery," I scolded her. "What is wrong with you?"

"Nothing."

"Thank you, Linda. Can you send him home when he gets back?" I asked.

"Sure thing, Lucy. Probably be home by supper."

"Oh, and please don't tell him I know he left."

Linda held up crossed fingers.

I thanked her again and took hold of Avery's arm to lead her from the cabin. It was a decent walk back and I still needed to finish the meal I had started.

"Do you believe her, Mom?" Avery asked as we walked.

"I believe she believes what she's telling us."

"What do you mean?"

"I mean, he could have just showed her the pictures and what she overheard him saying to Jeff wasn't about a birthday gift, it was about running away before my birthday."

"I don't know, I got a weird feeling."

"Your brother is fine. I believe that. If he did run away, it was because he was tired of his life here and didn't want to tell me. His senior year started two weeks ago. If he ran away, he went to your grandfather's."

And I truly did believe that. Jeff was a good man. He wasn't going to just drop a teenage boy off to fend for himself. Vincent had to have a plan that Jeff agreed with. I was certain when Jeff returned, he would tell me all about it.

But night came, dinner was done, and I hadn't heard from Jeff.

I passed it off as a dark walk to my cabin, one Jeff didn't want to take.

Although I wasn't fully worried, I stayed up way too late and fell asleep in the living room chair waiting for Jeff to contact me or Vincent to get back.

I woke up surprised that I hadn't heard anything and grew a little nervous. It was chilly, the fall air had set in and I should have lit a fire. Avery was still sleeping, and I figured I'd have some coffee then take the walk to Linda's.

I put the percolator on the stove, then while it brewed, I cleaned up and got dressed. Avery had woken while I poured my coffee. I took about two sips when I heard the voices outside.

It was unusual.

"What's going on, Mom?" Avery asked.

"I don't know." One more swig of my coffee, I set down my mug and walked to the front door, grabbing my jacket. I was full of worry. One person outside was normal, but it sounded like more.

I placed on my coat as I opened the door.

Mr. Parson was there, along with Linda a couple others.

I knew the look on Linda's face, I carried that look.

"What's wrong?" I asked.

"Lucy." Mr. Parson stepped to me. "Jeff never came back last night."

"I thought maybe he had car trouble," Linda added. "Sometimes that truck gives him a hard time. But he has never been this late."

"Is it possible," I asked. "That maybe he drove Vincent to St. Louis to his grandfather's. Maybe he fell asleep."

Linda shook her head and shrugged her shoulders.

"It's more than that," Mr. Parson said. "Your car you have on the ridge. You think it will start after all these months?"

"Yeah." I nodded. "I start it once a week, let it run. Why?"

"When Linda told me Jeff didn't come back," Mr. Parson said, "I ran up to Al Roseman's place. He has that radio. He had to dig it out. We ran the antennae and called out. He couldn't reach anyone. He tried every radio call channel. Even the state police. Nothing."

"Maybe the radio isn't working," I suggested.

"He got static. Just not a response."

Martina, an older woman who stood in the back spoke up. "Something is going on. I have a gut feeling something is going on. When's the last time any of us checked the news or tried to hear. We haven't. Heck, there could be an attack."

"So you want me to take a ride to Piedmont?" I asked.

"Either that," Mr. Parson said. "Or let me borrow the car."

"No. I'll go. My son is out there. I'm sure everything is fine," I said. "I'm positive Jeff will have driven Vincent to St. Louis and fell asleep at my father in laws. As far as contact, that radio probably didn't work and an attack on little Piedmont is highly unlikely. We'll take the ride."

I really was confident and believed what I had told them. I thought they were overreacting. The only thing I worried about was not only getting behind the wheel of my car, but facing civilization. Neither of which I had done in months.

EIGHT

BLEAK

For a split second I thought there was something Mr. Parson and the others weren't telling me. The way he handed me two rifles and ammunition, arming me and my daughter as if we were headed to danger. And Martina giving me a box with water and some food.

How long did they expect us to be gone? Piedmont at most was an hour and half drive.

"Is this really necessary?" I asked, staring at the weapons in the hatch compartment of our small station wagon.

"Is it necessary to keep them back here?" Mr. Parson asked.

"As opposed to having them upfront?"

"Lucy, keep them handy. You never know what you're running into."

After a slight huff, I took the rifles from the hatch and placed them in the backseat next to Martina's box of rations.

I had learned from Mr. Parson how to load and shoot a rifle, but I wasn't that good. Avery was better and Vincent was actually a great shot. Thankfully, I didn't think I'd need them.

"One more thing," Mr. Parson said then reached down to another box on the ground. From it he lifted what looked like a little radio. An old one from the eighties.

"Is that a CB?" I asked.

He held it in his hands, the wire to the microphone dangled over his hand. He lifted it and blew. Dust flew out. He coughed. "Yep. Al gave it to me for you."

"Does it work?"

"It should. I mean we didn't test it." He showed me an antenna with a suction cup on the bottom. "This goes on the dash near the windshield. And the radio, it plugs into the cigarette lighter."

"The cigarette lighter?" I asked.

"Damn it, it's an empty hole now for power."

"The twelve volt."

"Yes, whatever, watch." He opened the driver's door and slid in.

I watched from outside as he plugged in the radio, resting it on the console. Then he licked his fingers and moistened the bottom of the antenna suction cup, slamming it to the dash.

I gagged a little.

"There." He lifted the radio. "Oh, look it turns on. Now to put it on that station." He fiddled with the dial, rested the radio back down and lifted the microphone. "Al, come in."

"Supposed to say breaker, breaker," Al replied over the radio.

"Oh, I am not. Just testing it."

"Got ya."

"Good." Mr. Parson balanced the radio and microphone and got back out of the car. "Lucy, make sure you let go of the bottom to hear us and press it when you want to talk."

"Okay, listen, I appreciate this all, but it's a bit much. We're only going down to town," I said. "Find out if anyone seen them and we'll be right back. All of this is unnecessary. You guys act like we're headed into Red Dawn."

Avery asked, "What is that?"

Mr. Parson shook his head. "We're covering bases with you. The road is winding. This car hasn't been driven in a long time. If you get stuck, you need that box of food and water and that compass to make it back. That radio will let us know if you need help. So we aren't preparing you for war, we're preparing you for getting stuck."

That made more sense. Yet, hearing his words made me slightly angry with myself for not thinking about it.

The only thing I prepared to take for my trip into town was my coffee and a little bit of money in case I needed it.

Although I doubted the radio would work once we got off the mountain.

I thanked Mr. Parson, and Avery and I got in the car and began the journey.

He told us about a restaurant and hotel not far after we reached the highway. We could possibly stop there and call the sheriff if we wanted to.

I'd keep that in mind.

I was nervous at first. Not driving very fast. It felt almost alien to get behind the wheel after all that time. But it came back within ten minutes.

The last time we had been in Piedmont was when we passed through on our way to the cabin, stopping at a little diner for our last restaurant meal before going off the grid.

There wasn't much there. A small, one stop light town with older buildings paying homage to an era gone by and a sign that boasted the Ozark Heritage Festival. My plan was to head to the police station to see if there was an accident or if anyone had seen Jeff.

I was certain they knew him as he came into town regularly for supplies.

We followed the winding road from the community. I wondered if Avery was looking out the window for signs of the truck. I know I was.

"Are you okay?" I asked her.

"Yeah. Just thinking."

"About?"

"What could have happened?"

"What happened was simple. Your brother packed up. He went somewhere and Jeff drove him," I said.

"You're not worried?"

"No. Well, yes. But I don't think anything bad happened to Vincent. I don't." I said that with confidence and believed it because in my heart and mind there was no way fate would be so cruel as to throw us into something as horrible as the terror attack, kill Ted, and then a few months later, take my son.

No way.

It had been so long since I had driven those wood lined roads that I found myself having to give my full attention to the drive. Plus, I was driving a reverse direction than when I went to the cabin. A single winding road that led to a narrow one which eventually brought us to Highway Hh. The main road, where going east would bring us to Piedmont.

I was so consumed with driving I didn't notice, nor would I notice if anything was wrong.

"Lucy, come in. Lucy are you there." Mr. Parson's voice came over the CB.

It startled me and made me jump. I wasn't expecting it.

Avery lifted the microphone. "We're here. We just got to the highway. We'll let you know when we get into town."

"You have that address?" Mr. Parson asked.

"We do. We'll be there soon."

Avery didn't know how to end the radio call, it was awkward and new to her. She was funny, she started setting down the microphone, but stopped, lifted it to her mouth and said, "Bye."

It wouldn't be long before we got back to Mr. Parson.

I knew we were getting close to Piedmont when we passed signs for Clearwater Lake.

"There's a resort up ahead," I told Avery as we passed the sign. "Nine miles. That must be the one Mr. Parson told us about. Did you want to stop there or keep going into town?"

"Where are the cars?"

"I'm sorry?"

"Mom, we've been driving over an hour. I haven't seen another car."

"Oh, we did."

"When?"

"What?" I laughed. "Avery, I am sure we passed a car or truck. We just didn't pay attention."

"Okay, so let's look for one."

It was ridiculous. Of course, there were cars. Who notices if another car passes them or not. Other cars and trucks on the road are second nature.

So, to appease my daughter, I resolved to point out the next car we passed.

When a mile went by and we didn't, I attributed that to the area.

We kept driving, and sure enough, I didn't see another car.

It started to freak me out, scare me even just a little.

"Where are the cars?" I whispered.

"See," Avery said. "Something is going on." She reached for the radio and turned it on.

No music, no noise. I watched the numbers scan through quickly, never stopping, never finding a signal.

We passed the sign for the turn to the resort, but I kept going.

I just wanted to get to town.

The lack of signal on the radio I could explain to being out of range, but I couldn't explain the lack of cars or any road traffic for that matter.

My daughter was right. Something was going on.

But what?

NINE

PIEDMONT

First there was the red oak, engraved sign that read 'Welcome to Piedmont' followed shortly by the white sign with red lettering that announced that the Piedmont Chamber of Commerce welcomes you to the home of the Ozark Heritage Festival. As if Piedmont was this huge, bustling town, instead of the home of two thousand or so people.

If I had remembered correctly if I blinked, I missed the town square.

It was up ahead and as soon as I passed the chamber of commerce sign on the side of the road, I stopped.

"Mom? What is it?"

It took me a second to register what I saw and how I was going to relay it to Avery without sounding strange. "We just passed a Chick-Fil-A. Middle of the day, not a Sunday and not a car in the line. When have you ever known there not to be a line at Chick-Fil-A."

"Then you agree. Something is wrong."

"I believe that now."

I started driving again, staying slow, staying alert and looking around as I did. There were other businesses on the road, like

McDonald's and Sonic, yet they had no one there either. There was a supermarket, a couple cars were in that lot, but no one outside. No one loading their car.

Being daylight, it was hard to tell if lights were on, but to me it looked dark.

After passing the Gas Mart we drove down the main street.

No cars. No people. Nothing.

"What's the name of the street the police department is on?" I asked.

Avery unfolded the sheet of paper Mr. Parson had given her. "West Green Street."

"Keep an eye out for it."

"Maybe we should just go back," Avery suggested.

"No. Why would we do that?"

"I'm scared."

"I know." I didn't want to tell her that I was kind of scared as well. The whole town had a ghost town feel to it.

My pace was slow enough to look around, to not miss anything. I didn't worry about an impatient driver behind me. No one was on the road.

The one and only light turned red and I stopped.

Over the steering wheel I peered around. The buildings weren't much and the stores weren't any major names, all mom-and-pop places.

"Where is everybody?" I asked.

As if it mattered, I waited for the light to turn green and proceeded. I felt as if I'd stepped into some sort of science fiction movie.

Not a soul to be seen. No movement at all. It was as if everyone in town just up and left.

"Turn here." Avery pointed to West Green Street. As soon as I turned the corner, I saw the single police car parked in the lot next to the station.

It was small police station, a couple steps led to the entrance, which looked like it belonged to someone's house. A thick brown door and in front of it a glass storm door.

We pulled in front of the station and parked.

Avery and I both stepped out at the same time. As we approached the small set of stairs to the front door of the station, I noticed the exterior spotlight over the door was on. It struck me as odd; I thought most exterior lights were on a timer or solar charger and turned off when the sun came up.

I reached for the storm door, finding it amusing that the police station had 'hours of operation' and a sign that read to call 911 during no business hours.

After opening the glass door, I reached for the handle of the one inside.

Locked.

I tried again, then knocked.

"Maybe they're still closed," Avery said.

I checked out the business hour sign; it read "Open: 7 a.m." It was way passed that. I pounded on the door again.

"Hello!" I called out. "Hello!"

I gave them a few more minutes and tried once more. When I didn't get an answer. I stepped away from the door. "This is nuts." Placing my hand on the railing, I looked around. "Avery, do you hear that?"

"What?"

"Listen."

"I don't hear anything," Avery said.

"Exactly," I replied. "There are absolutely no sounds. Nothing. Dead quiet."

TEN

FLESHING IT OUT

Piedmont, MO

Car doors open, I turned on the ignition to use the radio, because for some reason it wouldn't work without the car being on. I guess back in the CB days they didn't have rechargeable internal batteries.

"Can you repeat that?" Mr. Parson asked.

"No one is here."

"At the police station."

"Yeah, and everywhere else. The town is empty. Not a person on the street. No cars driving. In fact…" I paused and lifted my eyes to the rearview mirror to check on Avery who paced on the sidewalk behind me. "Mr. Parson, we didn't see a car the entire way here. And the Chick-Fil-A didn't have a line in the drive thru. There were no cars there at all."

"Then something definitely is wrong when there are no cars in the Chick-Fil-A drive thru."

"My thoughts exactly."

"Any sign of Jeff's truck?

"Not that I saw," I replied, again, checking on Avery, she headed off to the left. "Avery," I hollered out to her. "Stay where I can see you."

"I'm just going in the lot. Maybe the police car has a clue."

"Okay, good thinking."

"Lucy, do you think maybe Jeff saw the same thing and him and Vincent went to the next town to get help or something."

I lifted the microphone to my mouth. "That's possible. Because that's what I think I'm going to do."

"Can you stay put?" Mr. Parson asked. "Al's giving me his Dart. Martina and I are gonna head on down there. We'll meet you. Just hang tight."

"Sounds—" I abruptly stopped speaking when I heard Avery scream. "I'll be right back." The microphone dropped from my hand as I hurried from the driver's seat.

Avery screamed again and cried out. "Mom!"

I reached for the back door to get the rifle when I saw my daughter was fine. No one was around her. She stood in the lot by the police car. The squad car driver's door was open and Avery was a few feet away both hands covering her mouth.

"Avery." I ran over. "What's going on?"

She stepped back even more, speaking through her hands. "I saw him in there. I opened the door and…" she whimpered. "Mom."

A few more steps and I arrived at the car. I caught the horrendous odor before I even turned around and looked.

The smell was so bad, I too brought my hand to my nose. But it didn't matter. The smell made its way to me, but I had to look, I had to see what happened to him.

The male officer, still in uniform sat in the driver's seat. His belt still on, one hand on the bottom of the wheel. His car's computer was on, but nothing was on the slightly lit screen.

He looked as if he had pulled in for the night and died right there. Right where he sat.

But what killed him wasn't something normal.

Slightly bloated, his color was a mix of gray with some blue. He had dime-sized sores all over his hands, neck and face. They looked fresh, but they hadn't bled because there were no signs of blood.

If they didn't look so much like a sore, I would have sworn they were burns. The ones near his mouth seemed to have eaten away the entirety of his lips, exposing the officer's teeth and gums like a skeleton. His eye lids were also gone.

Knowing I had seen enough, I closed the door with my body, shutting out some of the smell.

I was far from an expert on dead bodies, but I knew whatever killed him, whatever caused his death, did so long before Vincent and Jeff drove into town.

ELEVEN

ONE STOP LIGHT

I sat there for a minute, radio microphone in hand, trying to figure out how to explain to Mr. Parson what we had found. Explain without causing a panic. I decided on not telling him until he arrived. I just asked how long it would be.

Since he knew the way and wouldn't be driving as slow as me, I figured he'd be in Piedmont with Martina in a little over an hour.

Avery had moved to the steps of the police station. She sipped from a bottle of water.

"Are you alright?" I asked.

She replied with a short, snappy "No," as if to say, what do you think? I disregarded her deliverance. What she saw was disturbing and being mouthy just wasn't her.

"Mom, I just want to leave. I want to go back."

"And I can't."

"Why?" she asked.

"Because Vincent is out here somewhere. I have to look for him."

"I'm scared."

"I know," I said. "Mr. Parson is on his way with Martina. Maybe one of them can drive you back to camp and the other come with me. Or I go alone, either way, I have to move forward to the next town. We know they came this way."

Avery nodded.

"Look, we know something happened here," I told her.

"But what?"

"I don't know." I glanced up to the police station. "That door is locked up. The nightlight over the entrance is on, so whatever happened, happened before seven in the morning. I'm gonna bet close to it. That was probably the officer coming into shift."

"Or leaving."

"Exactly. Which would explain why there aren't cars on the road."

"Do you think they're all like him?"

"Again, I don't know. But I want to find out."

"How?"

"Let's take a walk."

"No." She shook her head.

"There's a store a few blocks up. Maybe there's a newspaper."

"You think they printed a story about the end of the world as it happened."

"It's not," I spoke firm, "the end of the world. And I don't know. We have been off the grid for months. This thing could have been happening for a while. Maybe last month when Jeff came into town it wasn't a big worry. Who knows? We won't know just by sitting here."

"I don't want to go. Let's wait for Mr. Parson."

"Avery, I'd like to give him some answers and it's going to be an hour. I'd rather find out something."

"Mom," she whined.

"Avery, enough. Okay? Get it together because if this is something really big and bad then you have to deal. Right now, we can't look for Vincent without having some idea what happened. Now, let's go, you're stronger than this." I held out my hand.

She slapped hers down into it and stood. "When did you get so tough? Dad was the tough one."

"I've always been the tough one Avery, I just let Dad be the fall guy."

I wasn't lying, I was the tough one, but I didn't really let Ted be the fall guy. I just didn't want to be tough anymore. When I met him, I immediately handed him the mantra. The baggage I carried, that I was tired of holding. My entire youth was spent wanting to have a normal family of my own. I had that. I baked cookies and watched soccer games.

It was every bit of a young life I didn't have. By tough I wasn't meaning physically strong or intimidating, I spent my life being emotionally tough, damaged, but my kids didn't know any of that.

I vowed to be a great mom, there for my kids, supportive and loving. I wanted them to see me cry and show weakness, to laugh and be happy, even though it wasn't always easy.

My own mother was an addict. When I was nine, she overdosed in an alley in the backseat of a 'client's' car.

For years I was in the system, bouncing from one foster home to the next while children services tried to find my biological father. As if he would suddenly come out of the woodwork with open arms and say, "Wonderful. I'll take her and love her."

I was realistic. I wasn't a bad kid, I didn't get in trouble. The only reason I bounced was it was end of term for the current foster family.

Just before my fourteenth birthday, Mimi and Pips fostered me. They were an older couple, already pushing seventy. It was wonderful. I didn't get forced out, because they made up their minds that I was theirs. On my seventeenth birthday they adopted me. My kids never knew they weren't my real parents.

I loved them. But I carried my past, never understanding why I'd grown up with so much to shoulder. So much weight of hurt to carry. I didn't know why until the day of the terror attack.

It was like emotional Karate Kid training, wax on, wax off and it all kicked into gear when I needed it.

I need it again.

Something horrible had happened in Piedmont. Perhaps other places. But my focus in that moment was the small town we stood in that was barren and devoid of life.

Avery and I walked to the small market a block up the road. It was mainly dark, a few lights in the back, and the door was locked. We tried the gas station, that too was locked. The power was on though.

Every little store on the main street was closed.

Each locked store reiterated my belief that whatever had happened here had occurred overnight. Everything in town closed at ten.

"They could have all left," Avery said. "Maybe they got a warning and the officer stayed to protect the town."

"That's good thinking. Jeff and Vincent may have rolled through, saw it closed down and kept going."

"We could go house to house. Look for people or…or bodies."

"We could do that." I placed my hands on my hips and looked around. "I just wished a business or store would give us answers. Why must everything shut down by ten?"

"Not everything," said Avery.

I glanced at her with curiosity.

Schmitt's.

Muted by the daylight, I could see the sign was still lit up in neon colors above the bar and grill. I didn't hear a juke box. That was the crazy thing about Piedmont, there was no noise. Perhaps my daughter was right. Maybe everyone evacuated. There had to be an event, something on the news that we missed.

There were no cars parked on the street. Three were in the lot. They could have been from apartments nearby.

I was leery, almost a bit scared to push open the door. What if it wasn't locked and we walked into dead bodies? I really didn't want to put Avery through that.

"Stay here," I told her.

"Why?"

"I want to see first, okay?"

She nodded.

With a deep breath, I pushed on the door.

It wasn't locked.

Admittedly, I was scared and like a child, I closed my eyes as I walked in.

I took a whiff to smell.

It was pungent, rotten like the police car. I smelled alcohol and fried food.

I opened my eyes.

If I were to surmise what I saw when I stepped into Schmitt's Bar, come up with a single word, it would be chaos.

The scent of death wasn't there and there also wasn't a single person or body.

"Come on in," I called out to Avery. "It's fine."

It really wasn't.

While there were no people or bodies, there were signs that people had been there. Chairs were toppled, drinks spilled, some remained on the bar half consumed much like the baskets of bar food.

Everyone in that bar left in a hurry and at the same time.

Someone left their phone on a table. It was dead, but I took it. I'd find a way to charge it. Maybe that person received one last text that would tell me something.

What in the world would cause everyone to race from a bar? That was what it looked like, they jumped and ran. All while a police officer sat and died in his squad car outside a closed police station.

It didn't make sense.

The events of Piedmont were shrouded in mystery. Was it just Piedmont or did it extend farther? I banked on the latter because if there was something bad that happened only in Piedmont, the authorities would descend on the small town and it would be swarming with people.

Like the attack on the Biomass energy plant.

That dead phone in my hand had answers to give. I knew it and felt it. I also knew that if Avery thought outside the box and searched around, we'd find other answers as well.

TWELVE

NONE TO BE FOUND

With Mr. Parson's arrival not far off, we stayed in the bar and rounded up some food. I knew Avery was hungry. Although we had Martina's ration box, I really didn't want to touch it, not with the journey I had ahead of me to find my son. Who knew if there would be power out there, people, food or anything?

There was deli meat in the fridge for making subs and I made us a few sandwiches. The thought of taking time to have a meal at that moment, probably to some would be a strange thing to do in the midst of the mystery and death.

Not me. I was excited to find bologna. Living off the grid there are things that you miss.

You don't sit back and long for things. Something usually triggers a longing and when that happens it's usually something you had taken for granted before going off the grid. Like:

Walmart.

Starbucks.

Bologna.

It tasted so good and not an item I'd ever thought to ask Jeff to pick up. I thought about washing down the sandwich with an adult beverage but opted against it.

I wanted a clear head to try to think about what had happened.

It couldn't have been a coincidence that such a major terror attack occurred not long before.

It had to be an act of war, maybe the town was evacuated because it was close to St. Louis.

Then again, what happened to that police officer?

So many questions.

After we had finished our food, we walked back to the car. I figured we'd drive it to the Gas Mart and think of a way to get gas since there was still power on Piedmont and I'd need it for the trip ahead.

As if we're a normal day I pulled up to the pump and shut down the engine.

"Any ideas?" I asked.

And just like that, Avery popped over the glove compartment and pulled out my wallet.

I forgot I had placed it in there.

I opened it and pulled out the one credit card I knew wouldn't get declined if indeed the pump worked.

"Do you think it will?" I asked Avery.

"Might as well try."

I wasn't sure how they worked, if the pumps worked on Wi-Fi or telephone lines. There was still power and if by chance it wasn't something happening to the whole country, the pump working was a good sign.

I inserted my card and watched it run through the cycle. Processing, processing…It took a minute, but the words 'begin fueling' told me the card went through. It was good news on more than one front.

Piedmont and the area may have been an isolated incident.

As I watched the numbers roll by with the filling of my tank, I thought of that police officer. He definitely looked as if he had caught something, which then made me worry that we would be exposed.

What if there was a biological attack? Was the officer infected when he stayed behind and everyone left?

There were too many 'what ifs' for my liking and if my son wasn't out there somewhere, I would go back to the mountain.

The pumped clicked to a stop at seven and a half gallons, just as the old beat-up Dodge pulled into the lot and stopped.

Martine was driving and Mr. Parson got out of the passenger side.

"There you are," Mr. Parson stated. "We went to the police station, saw your car, and couldn't find you. Then we go back and it's gone. You had us worried."

I pulled the nozzle from my car and hung it back on the pump, then looked at my watch. I had no idea we'd spent so much time in the bar. "I'm sorry, we were looking around for answers. I didn't realize we were out of sight for that long."

"So, did you find it?" Mr. Parson asked.

"The answer to what happened?"

"No, the answer to where everyone went." He paused. "We did."

Martina probably had a last name, but I didn't know it. I knew her only by Martina, and had seen her about three times since we moved to Gideon. She lived on the edge of the off the grid zone, closer to Al Roseman than us. She stood out because she looked tough to me. No tough in a worn way, just like she didn't take anything from anyone.

She was what I envisioned a rancher from Montana looked like. An older woman whose age was hard to tell, so I wouldn't even guess. Always wearing jeans and a tee shirt and no matter the weather, she had that flannel overshirt on. She wore her silver hair short, but it was fuller with large curls.

She looked no-nonsense and spoke that way, too.

I followed them in my car through and out of town.

As soon as we turned right on to a major road, I began to wonder how they found what they did. Whatever it was. A mile later, Martina put on her turn signal and turned. It was a small bridge over a creek and as we crossed, I saw the sign for the high school.

Martina stopped.

I wondered why they were getting out of the vehicle.

Martina hung what looked like a man bag over her head, allowing the strap to cross her chest.

"What are they doing?" Avery asked.

"I don't know. Let's find out." I reached for the car door and opened it. I was just about to ask what was going on, when I saw they couldn't drive any farther.

The driveway was packed with cars. Jammed together all the way to the lot.

It was like some weird school event where way too many parents showed up. But that wasn't the case.

"How did you find this?" I asked.

Martina answered, "Just a hunch, go to big public places, churches. Tried here first, we hit the jackpot." She looked at Avery. "Sweetie, you may want to stay back here."

"It's not pretty," said Mr. Parson.

"You went into the school?" I asked.

"Not yet," Mr. Parson said. "I don't particularly want to, I've seen enough right here."

I wouldn't pretend to know what he was talking about; all I saw was cars.

"Do you need…?" I trailed off, knowing the answer to my question already.

Martina nodded. "I think to confirm what I suspect, we need to go through. I mean, I can go by myself."

"I'll go with you," I told her. "Mr. Parson why don't you stay back with Avery."

"I'll stay back with the girl. That's a good idea," Mr. Parson said.

Something he saw beyond the scope of the immediate cars was enough for him, I was curious and scared of what I was about to witness as well.

I had made it ten cars when I saw the first body. She lay on the ground on her side, the arm under her body extended above her head. And like the police officer, she was covered with those sores. Only she wore shorts and I could see they were on her legs. Her eyelids gone as well as her lips.

I grunted out an 'Oh' as the smell wafted my way.

"It'll only get worse, breathe through your mouth."

Why did anyone say that, as if breathing through my mouth really would make a difference?

"Here." She pulled out a paper mask from her satchel. "It's doused with oils but it's better than this. Still, breathe through your mouth."

I placed the white mask over my nose and mouth, it smelled like cloves. Not a great smell, and it really didn't block out the smell of death, it just mixed with it.

Then the sound of flies was overwhelming, the first sound I had heard in the town. And more bodies appeared. They were everywhere. In between cars on a speck that was open. We had to step over them to go forward.

I didn't want to talk to or say much. I followed Martina as she led the way.

The cars extended all the way to the front of the school. Where four state police cars were parked out front.

With the exception of the flies, it was quiet and I didn't hold hope that we'd find anyone.

Martina pulled out a pair of gloves from her bag, placed them on and opened the door.

It was cold inside. The air conditioning must have been running.

The hallways up and down were lined with people and their belongings. Some died sitting against the wall, some looked as if they were sitting and tipped over.

Martina paused by a man who was sitting up. Looking at him, the sores, one would think he suffered, but his phone was in his hand, he was holding it tight. Without a doubt it was dead.

Martina crouched down to the body of the man. She reached into her magic bag and pulled out another smaller bag, she then lifted the man's hand. She peeled the fingers from the phone, a long stringy substance that looked like rubber cement stretched from his hand to the device.

Just as it was, Martina placed it in her bag, then carefully examined the man, tilting his head, checking out his neck and finally opening his mouth. After she examined the sores, she shook her head. "Where have I seen this before?"

She stood, took off her gloves and grabbed a new pair. "I have to tell you," she said. "You are handling this remarkably well."

"No, really, I'm not. I'm so close to vomiting."

"You haven't yet. You won't." She placed that phone in her bag and kept walking.

"Where are we headed?" I asked.

"I need to see the gymnasium, the cafeteria, as much as I can."

"Why?"

"See if we can figure out why these people came here. It's not a church. People don't generally gather in a place that's not a place of worship unless they're told to. Like with a hurricane, a shelter."

"You don't think this was like a medical camp. Maybe a makeshift hospital."

"Nope." She shook her head. "There is nothing here to indicate that. Plus, that guy back there with the phone. He wasn't going to be playing on that contraption if he was sick. He died fast. All these people died fast. You wondered where they all went, the town. Here they are."

"All of them?"

"There were one thousand, eight hundred and some people in Piedmont according to that sign. I'm pretty sure," she said. "They're all here."

THIRTEEN

FOLLOW UP

I didn't vomit.

I held it together, held it in, and walked that entire school with Martina. I would be lying if I said I wasn't worried I would see my son there, but I didn't.

Thank God.

Martina made no more assumptions or observations out loud until we returned back to the cars.

"That bad?" Mr. Parson asked.

"Worse than we thought Paul," Martina said. "Everyone."

"Everyone? Everyone in Piedmont?" Avery asked.

"I'd bet my last corn pad that there's at least two thousand people in there. I stopped counting at thirteen hundred."

Hearing that caused me panic; I shot a hurried look at Martina. "You were counting *bodies*?"

"I was, as many as I could. One eighty-three before we hit the school," Martina replied. "Granted I lost count, so who knows? But I am certain they're there. And Paul, no check in line, nothing to indicate they were keeping track."

"So, it's like you said," Mr. Parson stated. "They were told to go there."

"But why?" questioned Avery.

"Whatever killed them, they knew it was coming," Martina replied. "They evacuated there, figuring it was safe. Some didn't make it, as you saw in the driveway."

Mr. Parson shook his head. "So, there is no way to find out."

"I wouldn't say that," answered Martina.

I looked at her. "That's why you picked up the phone."

Martina nodded. "We charge it and find out what he was so busy on that phone for. Obviously, they rushed there to be safe, so why was he on the phone? Texting or calling someone. At least I hope he was. What he conveyed in those final messages could be so helpful."

"The grocery store probably has chargers," Avery said. "We can stop there."

"It's completely dead. Not sure it will charge again," Martina said.

"It will," I added. "It'll just take a bit to get enough charge. But it will."

Mr. Parson asked. "And if doesn't give answers?"

"Even if it does, we have to keep going," said Martina. "She has her boy to find. We need to find Jeff. We need to make sure whatever is happening out here isn't gonna touch Gideon."

Avery whimpered a little, "But if it's a virus, how can we stop it?"

"It's not." Martina shook her head. "It's not like any virus I have ever seen before. Whatever it was killed these people like this." She snapped her finger. "Tore them up too. But they knew it was coming, so how?"

Mr. Parson shrugged and shook his head, tossing out his guess. "They knew it hit elsewhere."

"So why did my son and Jeff keep going?" I questioned. "Why didn't they come back?"

"I don't think they found the school. I think they saw an empty town and kept going," said Martina. "Your boy don't drive or wasn't driving. I know Jeff. He kept going."

Mr. Parson nodded. "He'd want to know what happened before coming back so he could warn us."

"So do I," Martina said. "But I don't think it's safe for the girl to be here. I think she needs to go back home" She faced me. "If you want to head back, too, I can make it on my own."

"I want to find my son. Avery," I stepped to my daughter. "I know we talked about it. Is it okay if I go look for Vincent?"

"I wish you wouldn't."

"I know. But I have to."

"And I need to let everyone know what we found," Mr. Parson said. "I'll take Avery back. You two take the radio, keep in touch. Let us know."

I hated the thought of leaving Avery, sending her back up the mountain without me, but I also knew the mountain and Gideon was the safest place she could be.

At least for the time being.

I needed to find Vincent, and Martina, like the rest of us, was on a quest to find answers.

What happened in Piedmont would undoubtedly affect us one way or another and we needed to be prepared.

The best way to do that was to go forth and find what we needed to learn and hopefully find my son as well.

FOURTEEN

THE FIRST BLOW

My mind went to what happened. Not what happened in Piedmont or the rest of the world, but what happened that one day in Steubenville, Ohio.

I realized when I avoided the news, I avoided knowing what occurred.

Surely, in the time that passed they figured out who had done it.

Maybe that would give us an idea.

Before we parted ways with Parson and my daughter, all of us went to the grocery store.

The first thing Martina said was, "I knew it. Look at these shelves. The people were in a hurry. They didn't even stop to panic shop."

"They dropped their drinks at the bar as well," Avery added.

"An evening attack, night actually," I said. "So how did they get their warning, and know what to do?"

"The phones. Televisions," Mr. Parson answered.

Martina and Mr. Parson loaded up on supplies for the road and to take back to Gideon, Avery looked for a charger, one for the car, and I went to the magazine section.

I was hoping one of the big serious magazines did an exposé on Steubenville.

I didn't hold much hope in finding an article—it had been months and I doubted it was even still on anyone's minds—but I was determined to look while the others did their 'shopping.' To my surprise, there was one of the big news magazines and on the cover was a dark, dramatic image of a building engulfed in flames. The yellow lettered heading, read, 'Global Terror Attacks Remain a Mystery.'

I lifted the magazine, intent of skimming the story first, but realized it was almost an entire magazine dedicated to it.

A few flips of the page I saw Steubenville, then something in Amsterdam. I closed the magazine, looked around the rack for others, and when I didn't see any more, I took it.

"Either of you know about this?" I found Martine and Mr. Parson, they walked side by side in the store, each pushing a cart.

"What is it?" Mr. Parson asked.

"Apparently, after Steubenville there's been a bunch more attacks. I didn't read it, but judging by the headline, no one knows who is behind the terror attacks."

"Sounds strange," Martina replied. "Terror hits are all about attention. I don't get the news or follow it. Are they all different types of places or similar to the one you were in?"

"I don't know. I have this though." I lifted the magazine. "I intend to read it."

Mr. Parson looked at Martina. "I wonder why Al Roseman never mentioned that. I mean, he does give us the news when it's big. Surprises me he didn't."

"Or..." Martina looked at me. "Your son for that matter."

"My son?" I asked. "Why would my son know anything about the news?"

"He was always on that phone up by Al's property. I figured he went there to get a signal," Martina said.

"Are you sure it was a phone?" I asked. "Maybe he snuck that game of his."

"I'm sure it was a phone," Martina said.

"I cancelled all our phone services." I shook my head. "He was probably playing a game."

"Maybe," Martina said. "Or maybe he left because he wanted to find out more. Not worry you until he had answers. Jeff's wife said he had a bag with him."

"No." I shook my head again. "My son doesn't hide things like that. Jeff's wife also said he was making a present for my birthday. But who knows?"

"I found three types," Avery announced as she entered the aisle. "That way if you find any other phones you can charge them."

"Avery," I called her name. "Did Vincent have his phone?"

"No," Avery replied.

"Are you sure?" I asked. "He didn't have his phone?"

"I saw him with a phone," said Martina. "No one is in trouble, we are just trying to figure out if he knew ahead of time about what happened here. Like maybe he picked up the warning."

Avery chuckled. "And ran to help. No, not Vince. He was very self-centered. If anything, if he heard it, he went to say he survived it."

"But he didn't have his phone," Martina stated again.

"I saw him on the phone. You're sure?"

"I'm sure he didn't have his phone." She shifted her eyes to me. "You disconnected them. He did have a phone that Sonya gave him and paid for."

All three of us blasted a "What?!"

"She got him a phone. He kept it at Jeff's. Jeff would charge it for him and keep it quiet on the condition that if Jeff needed to use it, he could. He didn't tell you, Mom, because he didn't want to upset you. He knew how much you wanted to be there."

"But he didn't," I said sadly. "Is that why he left?"

Avery shook her head. "I don't know. He never once said he wasn't happy. I mean he was making money and..."

"Wait. What?" I asked. "He was making money? How?"

"He writes for a site about a city boy now living off the grid." She looked at Martina. "That's probably what you saw him doing."

"Why didn't you tell me?" I asked.

"He asked me not to. He's my brother."

"Fair enough," said Martina. "Sibling secrets are worth keeping."

Mr. Parson lifted a finger to get attention. "Where was the money going? How was he getting it?"

I saw the hesitation on Avery's face and took a guess. "Sonya."

Avery nodded. "She had an account for him and when he needed money, she'd wire it here and Jeff would get it. But that was only a few times. Don't ask me about the trading cards, I don't know why he took them."

I huffed. "Sonya. Has he been talking to her?"

"Uh, yeah. He loved her. I mean he's in love with her."

"She like thirty-five. He's seventeen!" I blasted.

"He'll be eighteen next month."

"Doesn't matter. She's not in love with him, is she?" I asked.

"I don't think so."

"If she is," Mr. Parson said. "Things happen."

"It's against the law," I shot back at him.

"Technically it's not," Mr. Parson said. "Missouri age of consent is seventeen."

Martina asked, "Do you think he just went to get his money or maybe he went to find her?"

"I don't know."

And I didn't. There could be lots of reasons my son took off the day before, but none of that mattered, it really didn't.

The next step to finding out anything was getting to the next town.

Poplar Bluff.

FIFTEEN

KNOWING MARTINA

It was a strange conversation that led to the discovery.

Loading up the cars, Martina looking around town to see if there was anywhere else we could break into and loot for our own good.

When we left that grocery store, it was also goodbye. We were separating.

Standing on that sidewalk, I said goodbye to Avery. Holding her, not wanting to let go.

Mr. Parson thought it would be a good idea to have her stay with Al Roseman and his wife. That way Avery was close to the radio and I could reach out.

I didn't think I would be gone long. I figured no more than a day or two, but by the number of items that Martina put in the hatchback of my small station wagon, I wondered if we were going to be gone for months.

Our plan was to make the next stop a bigger town called Poplar Bluff. I didn't understand why. It was the complete opposite way from St. Louis. That was where I believed Vincent was headed. Back home to his grandfather.

Martina believed he was going after Sonya.

I wasn't buying it. I countered with it being a ridiculous notion considering Sonya was from Hollywood.

Jeff wasn't taking him all the way there. Maybe to St. Louis. Not to Hollywood.

"How far is Nashville?" Avery has asked.

"Nashville?" Mr. Parson barked. "That's got to be about four or five hundred miles from here."

"Why would you say Nashville?" I asked.

"Because she isn't from Hollywood, Mom," Avery replied. "She's from Nashville, she does that singing show and reality show there."

"How convenient," Martina commented. "I mean, not far at all from here. Compared to California."

"It's a big guess," I said. "I really don't think my son is chasing some movie star."

"I have a good gut instinct. I know how teenage boys think, heck, I know how boys' minds work," Martina said. "That boy is going after that woman. Maybe he needed to sell the trading cards to catch a bus there."

"If he sold his trading cards it could have been anywhere, but it wasn't here."

"What makes you say that?" asked Mr. Parson.

"Because everyone was dead when they rolled through here yesterday morning. They left Gideon yesterday morning, which means they got here early, saw the town was empty and moved on."

"I think it happened last night," Mr. Parson said. "I think they came through here before it all went down."

"The bodies," I commented. "The police officer was awfully decomposed."

Martina added, "The bodies in the school were not. Elements, the heat, being in a car. No, I mean, I think it happened last night."

I whimpered a gasp and my heart sunk to my stomach. "Oh my God, they could have been caught in it."

"Mom, if it happened last night, they were long through this town."

"Why didn't they come back?"

Martina huffed. "Hog tie me to a mailbox, girlfriend, he went after the famous chick."

"What does that even mean?" I asked. "Hog tie you to a mailbox?"

"Look." Mr. Parson held up his hand. "There is one way to find out if he stopped here and sold them here."

"How?" I asked.

He pointed across the street.

I hadn't seen it before and if I did, it didn't register.

The Trading Stop. With a sign that said, 'We buy, sell and trade collectibles.'

Another broken window in town. The older folks with us were just leaving a trail of destruction.

We went into the dark trading store. It had collectibles everywhere, from magazines to toys.

Martina went behind the counter while I went into the back office.

Mr. Parson and Avery were just shuffling around, looking at things.

"Found something!" Martina yelled out.

I left the office.

Martina stood at the front counter, a ledger book open before her.

"A ledger?" I asked. "All the tech and stuff and they use a ledger?"

"Look at this place. I don't think the owner cares about computers. Here." Martina turned the book to me. "V. Carver? Is that your soon?"

"Maybe."

Martina shook her head. "One hundred and forty-two baseball cards, lists the years here from 1968 to 1975."

"Mom, that's him." Avery rushed over.

"Looks like they paid him five hundred dollars at eleven a.m.," Martina said. "He took that money and ran."

"Let's just stop and think for a second," I said. "Everyone in this town headed to the school for protection from whatever. If you guys are right. Vincent and Jeff would have long since been out of this town. Even if they went to Nashville, Jeff should have gotten back."

"Nope." Mr. Parson shook his head. "Maybe in the morning. But he wouldn't have driven those roads at night. I know my nephew."

"Okay, you said that twice," Martina said.

"Maybe it's not this celebrity," Mr. Parson said. "Maybe...maybe it was Jeff."

"Huh?" I asked, confused.

"Jeff is closer in age to Vincent, they spent a lot of time together. Maybe it wasn't the celebrity, maybe it was Jeff. Maybe they run off," Mr. Parson said.

"Stop." Martina held up her hand. "That don't matter. We know the boy came through here, collected that money and kept going. But that ain't the mystery I am setting out to solve. Something killed these people in this town. For the sake of all of our people, we need to find out what that was. What happened? I think, searching for the boy will give us the answers we need."

"So, forget speculating what happened to Vincent," Mr. Parson said. "Focus on what happened to these people, and we'll also find out about the boy?"

Martina nodded. "I hope."

Martina wanted answers to what occurred. I wanted answers about my son. A road trip we'd take together, with two different goals in mind.

"Tell me about Steubenville," Martina said almost immediately when we got in the car.

My mind was still on Avery and how I sent her back to the cabin with Mr. Parson. Not that I didn't trust Mr. Parson with my child, I just hated leaving her.

"I really don't know much," Martina said as she cleaned off the phone she'd taken from the dead man's hand. "I know something happened in Steubenville. An attack."

"You know as much as me."

"We have to undo the radio to charge this." She reached down and switched the radio power for the charger. "There." She set the phone down. "Everyone in Gideon has a story. Lots of people go off the grid for many reasons. Some just to be closer to nature. Some escape because it's better out of the city and to be more self-reliant. Like I said, everyone has a story. We don't like to pry too much unless we think you're a murderer." She smiled awkwardly. "Which you're not. But we know whatever happened there, took a lot from you."

"It was the aftermath. The press, the internet. My son saved Sonya, so our family became front page news and my husband's face became the poster child for the attack. I couldn't watch the news, go to the store, anything without seeing it. Being bombarded. But I never intended for this to be long term. More, healing. The last few months just flew by."

"Time does get away from you," Martina commented.

"Especially with the Gideon Garden in full bloom. I was always, like, after the corn, or after the tomatoes, we'll go. Then it was after the squash. Now I think I have potatoes."

"You do. And you're learning very well."

"There were books. Not sure why Mr. Gideon needed books. But they helped." I glanced over to Martina. "What about you? How long have you been at Gideon?"

"Fifteen years. Off the grid, I tried to do before, back home in Montana."

"Huh" the word escaped me in a 'you don't say' manner.

"What was that?"

"I figured you for a Montana woman."

Tightly closed mouth, she nodded. "I loved it there. I lived just on the outskirts of Billings, then moved to Roscoe, worked a ranch there about twenty-two years ago."

"I never heard of Roscoe."

"It's small. Very little population," she said. "Mainly it gets a small tourist drive. I mean I really thought it was the perfect place. It wasn't. Then Mr. Gideon reached out to me. He knew what I was trying to achieve and knew I was failing."

I listened to her talk, trying to figure out the why of her needing to get off the grid.

"So, you've been escaping civilization for over twenty years."

"Yep. Like you I was hounded. The press. People. We have similarities. Just a few things."

"What…what happened?" I asked. "I mean, you don't need to tell me."

"No, it's fine. I was a doctor. Obstetrician. My husband died, oh, gosh, now going on thirty years. I was a young widow, and I was devastated." She whistled softly. "It's no excuse, none. My mind wasn't there and I missed the blatant signs of preeclampsia in a patient carrying twins. I just refused to see it for some reason. And I lost all three."

I hid my gasp.

"Not only was it the state's biggest malpractice suit, but I was sued and prosecuted for wrongful death and served five years in prison as well. It followed me. People couldn't believe I was out of prison. Well, you can guess the story."

"I'm sorry. I'm sorry about it all."

"Thank you. Sometimes I wondered if it was me. Was I looking to see if I was followed, was I really followed?" She shrugged. "Whatever it was. I found peace at Gideon."

I was ready to comment, to say something else. I couldn't believe the hard and tragic life she had lived for the last thirty years.

The slight vibration buzz caught my attention and I glanced down. "We have a charge."

Excitedly, she lifted the phone and powered it up. "Oh, shit."

"What?"

"It's locked." She dropped the phone, shaking her head. "Might as well put in the radio again."

"The phone was a really great idea," I told her. "I didn't think, neither did Avery, that it was locked. Never crossed my mind. Next time though…we'll know."

"Maybe we won't have to worry about a next time," she said. "Maybe Poplar Bluff will give us the answer without having to snatch a phone from a body."

I hoped she was right. It wasn't that far of a drive to Poplar Bluff, and I really wanted to get some answers. But for as much as I wanted to believe that outside the city limits of Piedmont, everything in the world was fine, I knew it wasn't.

I think we both did. We were both fooling ourselves with wishful thinking.

Our drive took us on a highway, passed houses and small businesses and not once had we seen another car. That told me more than anything.

SIXTEEN

THE NEXT STOP

Poplar Bluff, MO

We entered Poplar Bluff, north of the town. It had a population the size of the borough where I lived, but had a bigger feel.

The four-lane road brought us first through the hotel district. Numerous motels and hotels for weary travelers coming off of the highway.

That alone told me that strangers in a town weren't going to be in the know or personally told what to do like the folks in Piedmont.

What went down in Poplar Bluff was much different.

That was confirmed when we drove by the Kroger. Windows were smashed, carts strewn across the lot. It was littered with items. People panicked and, in a rush, hurriedly emptied the shelves. At least that was what I thought.

"What now?" I asked as I drove. "Which way?"

"Follow the road. But drive slowly and keep your eyes peeled."

"For?" I asked.

"Anything. People. Signs." She shrugged. "I don't know. I feel it hit here at night, too."

"Why do you say that?"

"The smashed windows, lack of cars on the road. I really thought for something that hit fast, we'd see abandoned cars on the road."

My eyes shifted from watching Martina to watching the road. I didn't know what she was looking for. More than likely life.

It looked as if Poplar Bluff would hold no more answers than Piedmont.

"Let's pull over," Martina suggested. "There's a grouping of cars up there to the right by the Dairy Queen."

"That's a church next to it."

"I know."

I pulled as close as I could. It just like the high school in Piedmont. Cars just stopped and left behind while the occupants went elsewhere.

Martina put on her mask and gloves, offering me a mask as well. It was definitely in anticipation of what was to come.

We walked toward the church, weaving our way through cars and trucks. I looked in every vehicle I passed.

There was no one inside.

No bodies on the ground.

Wherever they were going, they made it. Unlike so many outside that school.

We made it to the front doors of the church without seeing a single body. It was a pretty good guess that the people went to church and not the Dairy Queen.

The ice cream store hadn't even been looted.

Martina had said something in Piedmont, that people sought God or something like that. We were about to find out if that was true.

The church was a brick church, more on the modern side if it was 1985. One single steeple above the single-story building.

Two burgundy doors were the entrance and they weren't locked. We pushed them open with ease.

Upon first view, and not first smell, it looked like Christmas service. Every pew packed with people.

The sun blasted through the two giant windows behind the altar, causing everyone to look like shadows.

The beams of light carried in the church, in it was dust and a million flies. As we walked up the main aisle, I saw some of the people were leaning on each other, all showing signs of that sore filled illness.

On the altar by the pulpit lay the man of the cloth.

I tried not to breathe through my nose, but even in my best efforts, it got me.

It wasn't just one body, it was hundreds. I didn't know how Martina handled it so well. But me, my moments as a trooper were done.

I immediately tasted the nasty stomach acid as it filled my mouth and crept into my sinuses.

Whipping off my mask, I thought about running out, but I couldn't hold it. I spun around and it erupted from my mouth. It was so horrible, I could taste the death as I stared at the body of a woman who sat at the end of the pew.

Her head rested against the arm of bench that formed an L at the end. Her lidless, lifeless eyes stared at me.

I felt guilty. Super guilty. Not only did I vomit in the house of God, but I puked at the feet of some poor woman who came to the church and took her last breath seeking salvation.

Even though she was dead, even though she was just a body, I still felt bad.

"I'm sorry," I said to her body. Then I saw it. The phone in her hand. "Martina."

I heard her shuffle over.

"What's going on? Whoa. Are you okay?" she asked. "That's a lot of vomit."

"Tell me about it. Look, she has a phone."

"Good thing you didn't get it wet, huh?" She reached for it. It wasn't as glued on with decay juices as the man at the high school. She lifted it, then reached into her bag for a pack of sanitizer wipes. As she wiped it off, it lit up. "Oh. I don't have my glasses on. How much battery?"

"Looks like twenty percent. Is it locked?"

"Yep. But…" She held the phone strategically in front of the woman's face. Martina smiled. "Facial recognition."

We took the phone out of the church and away from the bodies, continuously tapping the screen until we could open the settings and turn off screen lock.

There were a series of texts, between the church woman and a whole slew of people all within an hour of each other.

Someone named Casey referred to the church woman as Gi. We weren't sure what that meant, her personal information showed she liked to joke around, because her name in her Phone ID was listed as 'Gi, I wonder why.'

We saw that in the settings.

She was young, if the selfies in the phone were any indication, she wasn't any older that twenty-five. Still doing selfies in a bar with her friends.

While the texts have no real information as to what exactly happened, they told the story of desperation and of an event that was happening everywhere.

Mom, are you there?

Mom, I'm trying to call you.

Mom did it hit there?

Where did her mother live?

The poor girl was scared.

A text to John read, "*Did you get the warning? We just got it.*"

John replied, "*No. No one said anything about this area. I'm on the other side of the country though. We have to be soon.*"

"They're all like this." Martina scrolled. "I went back days to texts between her and her mom. Gi wasn't from here. She said she arrived and was stopping here for the night. She'd be home soon. And this John. What side of the country? So many questions"

I huffed in frustration.

"We need to plug in the phone and go back, emails, texts as far as we can. Two minutes outside the church only gives us a view. But it tells us what time it happened here."

"How?"

"At 10:52 p.m., Gi sent a text, "'*am at the church. Where are you? Hurry.*'"

And four minutes later, Casey texted, "*Are you sure it's safe. They said dark.*"

"What does that mean?"

Martina lifted her eyes to me. "I have no idea."

"What did Gi say back?"

"Nothing. That was it. So, we know her phone didn't die," Martina said, "so that means..."

"She did," I said, defeated. "Okay, where to now? Find a school?"

"We'll get to it. This is bigger than Piedmont. I say we keep moving around Poplar Bluff. Charge this phone. There has to be answers. We know they were warned. Right? So somewhere around here, we can find what they were warned about."

"What do you think it is?" I asked, as we got back in the car. "I mean, and don't get upset, but as a doctor, what do you think?"

"I think I'm wondering why you think I would get upset."

I started the car. "I'm sorry."

"Quit apologizing. Just tell me. Because of what happened, right?"

I nodded. "Yeah."

"I was sued, I went to jail, lost my license to practice, that doesn't negate the years of education and hands on I have. Despite my screw up, I will always be a doctor, or at least someone with the knowledge."

"So, what do you think it is?"

"Oh, I haven't a clue."

All that, all that explaining on how she's a doctor and she followed up with she didn't have a clue.

"I do know what it *isn't*," Martina said. "It isn't a virus. I mean, lethal viruses don't kill that fast. They invade and conquer, kill, and not in a few seconds."

"A weapon?"

"That is more of a possibility. But who? We need to read that magazine, see what we can pick up. If this is an attack, why Piedmont? Popular Bluff. They aren't significant towns. They aren't New York or—stop the car."

Her abrupt switch of topic instantly caused me to hit the brakes. Like someone calling out 'Deer.'

"What is it?" I asked.

She pointed. "Jeff's truck."

SEVENTEEN

ANSWER

We were headed south on Westwood Boulevard and Jeff's truck was on the opposite side of the road, a block after we passed the sign for the Poplar Bluff Middle School.

It wasn't parked, it looked abandoned, as if he swerved off the road some. His front end faced the parking lot of the Global Fitness Center.

It was hard to see if anyone was in the truck. My heart beat so strong I could feel it in my ears.

"How do you know that's his truck?" I asked, inching closer. "It could be anyone's truck."

"Could be. But last fall he hit a deer and he's been putting duct tape on that fender. That's what I recognize."

I stopped and put the car in gear.

"Stay here. I'll check," she said.

"No." I reached for my door.

"Lucy, they…they may be in there."

"Then I'll know. I'll know."

Martina waited for me, noticing my hesitation. I was scared. Why wouldn't I be? I didn't want to walk to that truck, look inside and possibly see my son. What mother would? But I was looking for my child and I needed to know the truth.

That twenty feet seemed like a mile. The ground felt unsteady, like miniature earthquakes going off at once. Then I realized it was me. I was trembling.

Within five more feet, I saw Jeff. His body leaned against the door. I knew it was him by that hat he wore.

I was stuck in my spot.

"I can't. Go," I told Martina. "Just go."

All my bravery was out the window. My stomach, hands, legs, cheeks, they shook. I could feel my blood pressure soaring, pulsing through my veins as I watched Martina approached the truck.

She didn't open the door. She looked at Jeff, slightly lowering her head then walking around to the front of the truck.

That lowered head expression.

It crushed me and a whimper escaped, making room for the heartache I was about to experience.

She disappeared from view and I heard the truck door open. She closed it briefly after.

"Vincent isn't here," Martina called out.

I gasped out almost a scream. All my boiling emotions exploded and I lost balance, dropping to the road.

"He's not there. Avery said he had a backpack?" Martina walked toward me. "No backpack in the truck." She held her hand out, helping me stand. "Are you alright?"

I nodded, unable to speak for a second. "Yeah, I uh…was it the same thing?"

"It was."

"People have to be alive. They have to be. Everyone can't be dead. We aren't. And where is my son?" I raised my voice as my emotions built.

"Lucy, Jeff's truck is facing north. He was headed north, your boy isn't in there. He took him somewhere. Dropped him off and was headed back to Gideon. I think I'm gonna give the truck a once over, see if there are any clues. Then we keep looking around town. Heck, maybe he's here."

I chuckled emotionally. "I don't think anyone is alive. It's so frustrating. Text message said something about dark. It was night. How much—" I stopped speaking and my eyes lifted.

"What? What did you think of?"

"Call it a hunch." I ran back to the car, opening the door.

"You move fast when you want to," Martina said.

I turned around holding the phone.

"Okay," Martina looked at me confused.

"That Casey person was the last one to text Gi. Right?"

"Right."

"Gi asked Casey where they were and to…" I glanced to the text. "Hurry. Meaning, she was expecting Casey to go to the church. Casey replied and never showed."

"Where are you going with this?"

"Just trust me." I found Casey's number and dialed.

Instantly, after barely one ring, a frantic male answered. "Gigi, you're alive. Where are you?"

I stuttered some, shocked that there was an answer. My eyes met Martina as I spoke in the phone, "Where are you?"

EIGHTEEN

HIDE AND SEEK

When my children were little, I swore there was an invisible person in my home called, 'Wass Sonme,' In fact, I named him that because he always seemed to be the culprit when anything was wrong, messed up or broken,

"Who spilled the milk?"

"Wass Sonme."

"Who left the fridge open?"

"Wass Sonme."

My children spewed forth the phrase and excuse, "wasn't me." So much it stopped sounding like they were saying that.

Talking to Casey was like talking to a six-year-old child. He refused to tell us anything. He was suspicious, and sounded nervous.

"Please tell us where you are," I begged.

"I'm not anywhere. Where is Gigi?"

"She...she passed, Casey," I told him.

"They got her."

"What got her? What is it?" I asked. "What is it that got all the people?"

"I don't know."

Again, I asked. "Where are you?"

"I'm, I'm just here."

"Where is here? Poplar Bluff?"

"Why do you want to know?" he asked.

"Because we're standing in the middle of a fucking street and everyone is dead."

"I know. But you are not my problem."

End of round one.

Huffing out an, "I give up," I handed Martina the phone. "You try."

Martina took it.

"Casey, hi. My name is Martina. I know you're scared," she said. "Can you tell us if there are others with you?"

"No," he replied.

"So, you're alone."

"No, I didn't say yes or no. I will not tell you. Are you them?"

"Them?"

"Them, the ones that did this."

"No."

"How do I know for sure you aren't lying?"

Martina shook her head and handed me the phone again.

"Casey," I said. "I am looking for my son. His name is Vincent."

"I don't know a Vincent and I don't know you."

What the hell was wrong with him?

Martina snatched the phone from my hand and ended the call. "Something isn't right."

"What do you mean?"

"That's not normal behavior. Something is wrong. He's off. I don't know." Martina shook her head. "Let me check out Jeff's truck. And whatever you do, if he calls back. Don't answer." She walked to the back of my car.

I watched as she took her rifle and loaded it, tossing the strap around her shoulder. She reached back into the vehicle, and retrieved the second rifle for me.

"Do we really need this?"

"Do you want to take a chance? Keep watch. I'll be right back."

I wanted to watch as she searched through the truck, to help her find something, but she was right. It was more important that I watch her back instead.

Whatever it was hit at night, but who knew what happened before that?

Things could have fallen apart.

I kept an eye out, listening for sounds, looking around.

A few times I checked on her, but couldn't see her too well. Occasionally I'd spot her silver hair moving inside the truck's cabin. It was unnerving and quiet on the road. Way too eerie. I nearly jumped from my skin when the phone buzzed.

It wasn't a call. It was a text.

I lifted it and saw it was from Casey.

"I'm coming for you," it read.

Something about it scared me.

Then I jumped from my skin again when Martina returned.

"I found something," she said. "Are you okay?"

With a deep breath, I showed her the phone.

"That guy probably lost his mind in all this. Can you blame him?"

"What do we do?"

"Leave. We're leaving anyhow. Get in."

I wanted to know what she found, but I wanted to get out of there even more. I got in and started the car.

"Where to?"

"Go straight. I found a receipt from a restaurant called Myrtles Place. The address is on the receipt. One burger, four beers. He cashed out a little after ten. It's hard to say how long he was there. But he was alone and there for at least a couple hours. Probably waiting to sober up before heading home. The restaurant is farther out of town."

"So, he stopped for a burger on his way back."

"That's what I think. Let's see if we can find the place; the power is still on here, maybe they have security cameras."

"Are you sure you were a doctor and not a detective?" I asked.

Martina laughed.

But I proved one thing, neither of us were any good without a map. We went round and round, unable to find the street it was on.

Finally, we passed it and instead of doing a U-turn, I went around the block. That was when it clicked. I saw it before but it didn't register. I thought at first it was some sort of school, it set down some from the road.

I stopped the car.

"What are you doing?" Martina asked. "Myrtles is a block that way."

"Exactly. Perfect place to stop for a beer after dropping someone off here." I pointed to the train station. "What do you think?"

"I think a teenage boy that sold his trading cards, trying to get to the love of his life or his pap, this makes sense. Great thinking."

We were like some sort of television detective duo. Trying to solve a double case, what killed the people and where was my son.

It was an impressive and newer building, perched in a finely landscaped area with newer steps that led down to the station. I pulled around the side street to get to the lot next to the building.

I pulled the car as close as I could and locked it for the first time in town.

Casey stayed on my mind, and I peered around to make sure no one was there. I doubted very much for as many turns as we made that anyone knew where we were.

I didn't understand why I was so scared. The dead can't hurt you.

If they could, we would be in trouble when we entered that station.

I could see the platform when we arrived and a train was there, and knew by the three bodies on the platform that it wasn't going to be good.

We went inside.

It was obvious people were trying to leave. There wasn't an abundance of bodies, not as many as the church, but they lay there, decomposing, blasting out a smell I would never get used to.

Martina stopped at a body. A woman waiting in line for a ticket. In fact, she was right there, first in line. Martina crouched down to her looking at her closely.

"This is going to bug me. I think I know what this is. But damn if it's coming to mind."

"It will. Like a name you can't remember, it will click."

"You're right." She stood. "Let's go to the other side of the counter and look," she said. "If Vincent got a ticket, he had to register his name and show ID. Did he have ID?"

"He had a license."

"Then he's in the system."

It sounded easy, no problem. Until we went around the counter. There were only two workers. One was dead on the floor the other died with her hand and face on the keyboard.

That actually worked in our favor, because the pressure of her on the keys kept the computer from going into sleep mode and password protecting.

It happened so fast and I could see that.

In her other hand was the driver's license of the woman on the floor. She was in the middle of adding information when she died.

At least it was quick.

I took comfort in knowing that if God forbid something happened to Vincent, if he got caught in whatever it was that was happening, then he didn't suffer.

Martina lifted the woman's head and hand from the keyboard.

Then came the hard part. We didn't know the program or how to even search. Neither one of us were very computer savvy. I tried to relate it to the banking software I used in my old job, a simple account search, but it wasn't yielding anything. I couldn't find a passenger manifest registry, if that was what it was even called.

Martina took over and told me to check the drawers and counters. Maybe there was a training manual somewhere.

The dead woman was on a rolling chair; Martina moved her aside and I went behind her to the counter.

I didn't even look on the counter at first, I checked the shelves and files. But if Vincent had left the day before I doubted anything was filed.

When I thought that, I saw the black bins with stacks of papers in each one.

I lifted the stack and looked at the top sheet. It was a printed passenger manifest for a bus that left at 10:05 p.m. for St. Louis. The one under had left five minutes earlier. "I found something."

"Me, too."

"I found the manifests for the buses and trains."

"I found the manifest search."

I didn't know whether to leave my find and go to her or look. So I just started looking at the names on each manifest. I made it through about twelve. Not finding Vincent's name at all.

"Is he going to be eighteen on October eighth?'

"Yes." I gasped and turned around. "You found him?"

"I did. He didn't take a train. He took a bus."

"To where?"

"Cairo, Illinois."

"What?" I asked shocked. "What time?"

"Bus left here at four. Arrived there at seven. Him leaving that early explains why Jeff was at that bar having a bunch of beers. Jeff probably was looking for an excuse to stay in town."

"So, Vincent was out of here hours before the event hit. How far is Cairo?" I asked.

"Actually, not far at all, if I'm not mistaken. Lucy, what's in Cairo?"

"I don't know. I haven't clue. I never even heard of it until right now."

"I guess we head to Cairo."

"Are you sure?" I asked. "I don't want to make you go anywhere if you don't want to."

"Lucy, for the sake of our people, we need to find out what happened. Might as well find Vincent in the process. We just have to figure out what is in Cairo."

"Like I said I don't know. But it won't hurt to find out if his sister has other secrets she's keeping."

"Hopefully she does."

I shrugged. I honestly didn't know. Like I said it was worth a shot.

I was going to ask Avery. Hopefully, the radio worked enough to contact her.

It made absolutely no sense, why my son went to Illinois. None. It wasn't close to our old home or his grandfather. It wasn't even close to Sonya.

My son was a mystery, as much as what wiped out the world.

I was just glad the path to solving one could actually lead to the path of solving the other.

NINETEEN

MORE THAN EGYPT

Avery wasn't any help at all. She never heard him mention Cairo, and I believed that when she referenced that it was in a foreign country.

She was quick to speak to because she was staying with Al and was right near the radio. Mr. Parson, however, was another story. We asked her to find him so we could speak to him and since we didn't want to take a chance on getting too far away from the signal, we waited until he came on the radio.

Waiting would put us in Cairo just before dark and that point it would hard to drive back.

When Mr. Parson picked up, I immediately told him that Jeff had passed. That whatever took everyone else's life took his as well.

He would convey that information to Linda personally.

"And there are people alive," I told him.

"Oh, thank God. So, people did survive whatever happened."

"Looks that way. Depends on where they were. Obviously, a church or school wasn't safe."

"I take it you found them?" Mr. Parson asked.

"Not really. We spoke to one man on the phone. We took a dead woman's phone. He answered."

"Did he mention what happened? How they survived."

"No," I replied. "But, the one guy we spoke to was acting strange. Like, I hate to use the word, but crazy. Wouldn't tell us where he was, or who he was with. He just said he was coming for us."

"Come for you to pick you up or come after you?"

"I don't know," I replied. "We didn't want to find out. We did find out that Vincent left Poplar Bluff by bus. We found a manifest with his name on it."

"So, he sold his cards for a bus ticket."

"And probably gas for Jeff," I said. "Yes. But in search of our answers, that's where we're headed."

"That is?"

"Cairo."

"Do you mean, Care-Oh? Cairo, Illinois?" Mr. Parson said shocked. "Heck, that's not even a hundred miles from Poplar Bluff. Why the heck did he need that much money for a ticket? Can't be more than a twenty to get there."

"You've heard of it?" I asked.

"Yeah, it's as small as Piedmont, but it's positioned where the two largest rivers meet. The Mississippi and Ohio Rivers. It's a ghost town."

"What do you mean?" I asked.

"Just dwindled. Population is down to the same as Piedmont. But it's spread out. It's sad. Is he taking a boat? Was there another destination on that manifest?"

"Just Cairo and I have no idea about that boat. I do know this: with the timing of all that's happened around here, Cairo was my son's last stop. I feel it. Good or bad."

"You do know he could be on his way home, right?" Mr. Parson said. "He could be making his way back to Gideon. Keep the faith."

Keep the faith. Encouraging words to end the radio call on.

My faith wasn't just challenged by my son, it was challenged by what I'd witnessed happen to the world already. It was scary and I wasn't sure it was even over.

<><><><>

Twenty miles before the town of Cairo, the radio cackled and hissed.

Surprisingly, it was Mr. Parson again.

"Hey, wanted to let you know," he said. "I told Linda about Jeff and everything you've found out there. She remembers Vincent talking about Cairo. She thought he was talking about Egypt."

"Doesn't everyone?" I asked.

"Not me," Mr. Parson replied. "Linda said it was a couple weeks ago she heard Jeff and Vincent talking. She said the way he talked, he was going to Cairo, without a doubt. Taking a plane. Again, she thought he was talking about taking an Egyptian vacation and thought it was cute, you know?"

I looked over at Martina. "Is there an airport in Cairo?"

Martina shrugged. "I don't know."

Putting the microphone back to my mouth, I asked Mr. Parson.

"Can't be a big one and no bigger or smaller than the string of municipal ones from here to there. Tons of little ones. Oh, wait, yeah. Very lenient airport. Think a few years they were fined by the FAA for not enforcing regulations."

"So, he wouldn't be catching a flight there," I said.

"Heck no. They're mostly crop and private planes that wanna fly under radar."

Martina hurriedly glanced my way. "Private plane."

I lowered the radio. "Sonya."

Our plan was to take Highway 57 all the way to Cairo, across the Mississippi, where it would bring us only a few miles from the airport. But that changed with a massive pile up that caused us to leave the highway and shoot to backroads. The fires still smoldered from the wreckage, the smoke seeping into the sky. One could only guess what caused it.

It happened in the midst of the event, because there were no police cars or firetrucks.

We had to find another way in.

Like my call to Casey, on a whim, I grabbed Gigi's phone. Strangely enough the GPS still worked, and once off the highway it took us on a country road that ran parallel to the Mississippi River. We only passed a couple houses and a business so it was hard to gauge if anything had happened there.

We still hadn't seen any moving cars.

The country road brought us in south of the city, where Missouri met Illinois, and Kentucky was a hop, skip and a jump over the Ohio River. We drove over a scarily narrow bridge, one I probably would have held my breath crossing had other cars been flowing from the other direction. The bridge crossed the river, then farm land, staying narrow for the longest time. After a closed down visitor's station, that was all boarded up, we finally saw some place with a sign about slot machines. I slowed down as we passed it, trying to get a peek at what I hoped might be some sign of civilization.

The glass on the front door was busted, as well as what looked like part of a neon sign, making me think this town went down long before the event.

We kept moving and I kept hoping to come into the town. I saw signs for Fort Defiance Park, but didn't see the camp itself.

I knew we were really south of the airport.

Cairo was small, so it wouldn't take much time to get through the town, but it felt like forever as we drove closer. Finally, after what seemed like an eternity of driving through nothing, we started to see houses and scattered buildings.

Rolling into Cairo wasn't like driving into your typical small town. There was no town square that defined it.

That's what made it stand out to me. There was a problem.

It was getting dark and I knew immediately, something was wrong.

It was off.

It wasn't like Piedmont or Poplar Bluff, where the town was basically unscathed and barren of people.

It was a disaster. But it wasn't a recent disaster.

Buildings and homes were vandalized, windows broken, and very few cars littered the streets. It was as if a riot rolled in years before, consumed the town and moved on.

Yards and lots were overgrown. We passed an abandoned medical center that looked like it was on the TV show *The Walking Dead*.

One other thing I noticed: there were no streetlights on.

They should have started to illuminate the roads, they didn't. No electricity.

What happened in Cairo that made it different?

Was this the way it was? Why in the world would Vincent go to a ghost town?

"This is sad," Martina said. "I wish I knew more about what happened."

"I just keep thinking, why would they come here?"

"Well, you heard Parson. Under the radar. She's a big celebrity, probably didn't want it to get out she was landing and picking up an underage boy."

"That makes so much sense." I reached down and put my headlights on. "I guess the power went out."

"Looks that way."

"Think we can see our way to the airport?"

"Yes. But, honey, it is possible, he flew in and out. We might be best served to stop for the night, grab a bite to eat, a have a drink, and first light hit that airport."

"Where at?"

"Map is showing a Comfort Inn a mile up the road. I'm sure we won't have a problem getting a room."

I don't know why, but that made me laugh. I know she wasn't totally serious. But it wasn't long after she said that, I saw the metal archway that extended over the road.

It read, 'Historic Downtown Cairo.'

As we crossed under I noticed they had tried to give the town a facelift. Newer, but old-fashioned lampposts lined the streets. The kind that looked like the gas street lamps from the 1800s, only they were all busted. Every one we passed had been broken.

So consumed with looking around, I slammed on my brakes when Martina called out, "Lucy, watch out."

Just a reaction but I was glad I did.

There was a line of cars blocking the street. They hadn't been abandoned, they were deliberately placed there. Like a barricade.

"Do you think they're protecting the town?" I asked.

"I think we need to back up, turn around and find another way."

"If we just go to the right—"

"I got a bad feeling. Turn around."

Placing the car in reverse, I looked in my rearview mirror, it was dark and the rear camera was showing nothing.

The only light we had was the moon, and that was clouded over.

I kept reasoning that it was too dark to be a roadblock. That everything was fine.

If there were survivors, surely we would see fires, or candles, or something.

But remembering we drove by a dollar discount store, I made that my goal. It wasn't the Comfort Inn, but it would be a place to stop.

I backed up to do a three-point turn and I saw the figure in the street. It startled me and I thought at first it was just my imagination, but Martina saw him too. I couldn't really see him properly. He was a shadow, just standing there behind us a good fifty feet.

Turning my head, I looked back to the line of cars blocking the road, wondering if I could just jump the sidewalk and go around, when I saw eight or so more figures emerge.

Again, like the male figure behind us, they were shadows.

Walking slowly.

My car wasn't moving, and I watched Martina reach to the back seat for her rifle.

"You think we need that?" I asked.

"I don't think we should take a chance," she said. "Finish turning around and get passed that guy behind us."

"Martina, maybe they're just curious to see. Maybe they're surprised that someone survived."

"Oh my God, you cannot be that naïve."

"What do you think they are?" I asked. "Bad people that are gonna attack us?"

"People protecting their town from strangers."

"They're survivors. They need to know we mean them no harm." I reached for the car door.

"Don't be an idiot, Lucy, turn around."

"Seriously? You just called me an idiot. Unreal." Shaking my head, I opened my door and stepped out.

I guess Martina thought it was better to join me than wait. She got out too. I looked over, she held that rifle. I wished she didn't.

"Hello!" I called out. "Hey, hi. We mean no harm. Are you survivors?"

No one replied.

"Lucy, let's go."

I looked at the people just standing there. I wished I could see their faces. But the way they stood there, they were assessing us.

"They don't have weapons," I whispered. "No one is holding a gun."

"How can you tell?"

How could she not? They stood there, shadowy figures of all shapes and sized. But they didn't say a word.

Not a noise.

Then the unexpected sound of running footsteps came our way. It didn't sound like a crowd, it sounded like one person running in the darkness. Their feet slamming against the pavement, echoing in the dark empty town.

Out of nowhere from my left, a younger man raced toward us. He paused only briefly only for a second before us. Looked at us with desperation as he spoke, out of breath.

"Run," he said, and he took off.

TWENTY

HIDEAWAY

A panicked young man running through the dark streets. Ominous shadow people standing in a line in front of a barricade.

I saw the look on his face. I thought briefly it was fear.

He said to run, I wasn't going to question him.

I believed him.

There was danger.

While Martina ran toward him, my first instinct wasn't to leave the car or our supplies. I could drive away just as quickly.

I spun around to return to my car and two steps toward it, I saw the man in the front driver's seat.

Whether it was the guy who stood behind us, I didn't know, but that split second look at his face would stay with me forever.

The maddening look in his eyes as my dash light illuminated his sore covered face, he looked at me then looked down. His hands moved frantically downward as if he were trying to break something.

"Lucy, come on!"

I heard Martina call. She was farther away. I turned from my car to peer in the direction they went. She was at least twenty feet ahead with that young man impatiently waiting for her to move.

The moment I started to run her way, I saw through the corner of my eyes, the people by the barricade ran toward me.

Martina moved slower, waiting for me, and I caught up. The young man led us through the alley for two buildings.

I looked back over my shoulder to see that we were being pursued.

At the end the alley the young man turned left, darted between a few cars and ran to a red brick building.

He stopped by a door, banged four times and it opened.

He stood in the open doorway. A blast of light came from inside.

"Hurry," he urged.

He looked beyond us watching.

Martina raced into the building, and as I crossed the archway, the young man grabbed hold of my arm, yanked me in and slammed the door.

Within seconds of bringing down the bar lock and latching the door, there was banging coming from the outside. Pounding against the door.

It took me a few seconds for my eyes to get semi used to the bright lights inside. Battery operated worker spotlights.

"Don't worry they won't get in," he said, then hollered. "Perry, the spotlight!"

"They broke it," replied another male voice. "I wasn't able to fix it before dark."

"Damn it." The young man shook his head. "They aren't getting in here. If they do they won't make it to the room." He pointed to the lights then led us away from that door. "This way."

He took a few steps and paused before turning the bend. "Is that loaded?" he asked Martina.

"Yeah. Are you going to ask me to put it down?"

"Nope."

A door was on the left as soon as we turned the bend and we stepped inside. It was a large room, probably once used for storage. No windows. There were seven other people in there: three women, a child about six years old, and four men.

"Where did you find them, PJ?" asked a man who walked up and closed the door, aiming his question to the young man that helped us. "Didn't think anyone else survived unscathed."

"They rolled into town. Not sure why, no one comes to Cairo," PJ replied and turned to face us. "Ladies, this is Perry. He owns this building."

"The street side of the pharmacy." He extended his hand to us. "I'm the pharmacist."

"Lucy," I introduced myself. "And this Martina."

Perry folded his arms. "So how did you survive or wasn't your city hit?"

When he asked that, I didn't reply because all I kept thinking was, *Thank God, we're gonna finally get some answers.*

"We weren't hit," Martina replied. "Of course, we're up in the mountains between Reynolds and Wayne County, Missouri, pretty remote and off the grid."

"Preppers, huh?" Perry asked. "Wow, bet you're loving this."

"We're not preppers," I said. "At least, I'm not. And being off the grid is amazing except for now. What is going on?"

"You don't know?" Perry questioned.

I shook my head. "No. Yesterday morning my seventeen-year-old son decided to take off. I went looking for him and this is what we came down the mountain to. We waited a day, thinking that him, and the neighbor that drove him just got held up, didn't want to drive back at night."

"And how did you end up here?"

"We followed a trail. He came to Cairo."

Perry whistled. "Cairo? Does he know someone here or was he smuggling?"

"What?" I asked confused.

"I don't mean drugs." Perry held up his hand. "Sometimes planes land here and they aren't all that official with who lands and who takes off."

"As a matter of fact," Martina stated. "Close. We think he was meeting a private plane that belonged to a friend of his."

"A celebrity?" Perry asked. "Or politician? They stop here a lot under the radar. Well, doesn't matter. Hopefully he flew out of here before it hit. You said yesterday? Was it morning he came, or afternoon?"

I answered, "He would have gotten here about seven in the evening."

Perry looked at PJ for a second then back to us. "Come on. Let's sit down. Are you hungry?"

"We had food," Martina said. "It's in the car."

"I tried to get the car," I added. "But one of those people chasing us was in it."

"He won't be by morning." Perry indicated to a small table and chairs in the far corner of the room. "Come on, sit. I'll see if I can fill in some blanks for you."

A little huff of air escaped me. A cross between a scoff and a laugh. "Blanks? Perry, we know nothing," I said. "It's *all* blank."

TWENTY-ONE

THE BLANKS

I couldn't recall if I ever had brandy, let alone out of a tiny little cup like they had at the dentist office, but I had some at that table, courtesy of Perry. Our meal consisted of Spam chunks, cheese and crackers. I was hungry and it tasted like I was eating in a gourmet restaurant.

The room was set up as a 'wait it out' place, it didn't look like they lived there. We seemed to be the celebrities and all eyes are upon us.

"I think it might be better," Perry said, "if you ask questions. Might help to get us started. But first let me ask one question, you don't seem like a mountain woman. Her..." He nodded at Martina. "Yeah. You. No. Then I could be wrong. But did you run to the hills because of the terror hit?"

"Yes and no," I answered. "I was in the Steubenville attack, and it was too much. We gained a lot of attention for some reason and I just needed to escape. Me and the kids. Escape and heal, shut off from everything."

"Probably saved your life," Perry commented.

Martina spoke up. "We saw a magazine. There were other attacks? The cover said something about it being global."

"Yeah, it wasn't like a world war," Perry answered. "It was six cities across the globe, all alternative energy sources."

I asked, "Did they find out who was behind it?"

He shook his head. "No. There are theories."

PJ interjected. "A lot of folks think it's aliens. Cleaning the planet up, making it work for them. Like a terraform. Hit the alternate sources so after they take what we have, we can't find something else."

"Aliens?" I asked. "Like outer space."

PJ nodded.

"That's a theory, right?" I asked.

"Yes."

"Yeah, not exactly a plausible one," I blurted in my sarcasm.

Martina faced PJ. "Any theory is a plausible theory, son. Especially if no one took blame or they didn't figure out who did it." She gave me a scolding look.

"I'm sorry," I apologized. "I'm so on edge. Is what's going on out there now all connected?"

"Oh, it has to be," commented Perry. "I mean it is no coincidence."

"Is it everywhere, all over the world?" I asked.

"That …" he waved his finger. "We don't know. However, try to call someone overseas or anything, there's no answer."

"It's the next phase," PJ said.

"The next phase?" I asked. "As if there are more?"

"I think, for sure," PJ replied. "If the alien theory is true."

With a nod and a hmm, I sipped my little drink.

"We found a phone," Martina said. "And it seemed as if the girl was texting people because there was a warning."

"Oh, there was," Perry answered. "It started four days ago. It swept across the continent, west to east."

"Following the wind," Martina stated. "That's a heck of a sophisticated weapon that it doesn't decimate with the wind."

"Sounding more and more like aliens." PJ nodded. "Doesn't it?"

It didn't. It wasn't even a consideration in my mind. I wasn't going to be sarcastic again toward someone who was not much older than my son. Curious, I turned to Perry. "Did the attacks stop before this, whatever it is, wind thing."

"No, the last one was just before," Perry said.

"Maybe it wasn't a weapon. Maybe," I said, "whatever is happening was what caused the attacks to stop. I mean, nothing creates anything more deadly than Mother Nature."

PJ laughed.

"What?" I asked.

"You think this is an act of nature?"

"And you think that's ridiculous?" I questioned.

"I do."

"The same guy who things aliens are coming," I snapped.

"Yes." He nodded.

Now it was my turn to laugh.

Martina held up her hand. "I'm gonna say it's a weapon. Perry, was there any indication something like this would happen?"

Perry shook his head. "No. We just heard news it happened here and there, then towns started getting warnings. They said go underground, airtight if possible, and after it passed do not go out for two hours. Ultraviolet light and, heck, any light made it worse."

"How did they know?" I questioned. "I mean was it a cloud. How could they predict it?"

"They said it was like a thin fog. Not dense which surprised me. Then again, spores don't need anything heavy to carry them."

Martina exhaled. "That's where I've seen it." She turned to me. "The lesions. When I saw them, I thought advanced Gardener's disease. Farmers and people working with soil would catch it from fungus."

"Gardener's disease?" I asked.

"Technically it's called, Sporothrix."

"Sporothrix lesions. Good call," Perry said. "I recognized the lesions right away, as well."

"What are the experts saying?" Martina asked.

"Nothing," Perry replied. "Once it hits a town, they go dark. Most dead. Hiding. So if there are experts out there working on it, I don't know about it. I grabbed my medical book, the big book, as I call it from my office upstairs. I'm not doctor, but I think it's meningeal and multiorgan disseminated sporotrichosis. The meningeal would be the only explanation for the crazies."

"The … crazies?" I asked. Out of everything he had just said that word was one word I understood.

"They're just sick, those folks out there. They were fine. Doug Harris is out there; he worked for me," Perry said. "He left our shelter here in the two-hour time frame. They got hit with the remnants, not enough to kill them, but it sure as hell, gave them the lesions and makes them a bit nuts. It took about three hours to get them to that state. It moves super-fast."

PJ added, "They'll be gone in by sun up. Lights irritate the hell out of the lesions, half those who were sick learned that the hard way and they retreated. We were ready tonight. Last night, we weren't. We didn't know how bad they were until they attacked my aunt,"

Perry slowly shook his head. "My sister, poor thing. They just attacked her like she was a threat."

I pointed backwards. "As they relentlessly pound at the door."

"This is all new to us." Perry stood, walked across the room to get the bottle. He brought it back. "Piecing it together." He refreshed our glasses.

"You're doing a great job at that," I commented.

"So, it is a weapon," Martina said. "It has to be. A supped-up fungus with an advanced delivery system."

I looked at PJ, lifting a finger. "Don't say aliens."

He shrugged.

"Perry." Martina spoke with question. "If it's fungal it can be cured. The ones out there, the ones that didn't die. Even this advanced, a topical for the lesions and intravenous treatment could help them."

Perry nodded. "Yep. Amphotericin B. I looked it up. I thought, take Doug and whoever to the medical center six miles out, find it there and treat them. But they won't let you near them. That's how my sister died. I read a case study, it can cause complete psychosis once it hits the brain."

"So, basically, there's no turning it back," I said. "Once they catch it, they're doomed."

"Unless we knock them all out and hog tie them, there's no curing them. Eventually, they'll all die," Perry said. He lifted his cup and took a drink, as a tear fell slowly down the side of his face.

TWENTY-TWO

IN THE DARK

We heard them scuffling and knocking things over, throughout the night. They were smart enough to figure out that there was another way into the building and even broke into the pharmacy. But they were too stupid to find their way to us.

Perry was nervous they would find it and Doug hadn't worked with Perry long enough to even know about it.

But *they* knew. They knew it was somewhere and that we were hiding, hoping they wouldn't find it.

It wasn't as if they lost their minds and become zombie-like mindless monsters, they were just determined and angry. They needed to get us. We were their enemy for some reason.

I wondered how much the disease would have to progress before they could no longer be brought back and cured.

Perry believed at this point it was already too late, but he would be willing to try.

Martina didn't say much, nor did she outright tell Perry she was a doctor. Maybe he figured it out, maybe he didn't.

I knew one thing for certain, if it wasn't for PJ, I shudder to think what would have happened to us.

Perry said his sister didn't think she was in any danger, she approached Doug, all was fine and then Doug snapped. He and three others, viciously beat her down until she was dead.

PJ was nearby, heard it, and ran but she was gone and they turned on him. He was fast enough to get away.

In fact, he was out and about looking for people, trying to stop someone from falling victim. He was on his way back to the hide out when he spotted us.

Martina was resting. She sat on the floor, back against the wall with her eyes closed. I wasn't sure if she was sleeping. I didn't know how anyone could sleep with the noise.

But we were assured they would stop at first light. Then they'd retreat into the shadows, like vampires. But they weren't. They were just sick.

I moved from the floor back to the table. I thought I'd have a bit more of that brandy. I was anxious about the next day, going to the airport. According to everyone, they didn't keep very good flight records so it would be hard to find out if the plane landed and left.

Surely, Vincent was out of town before this all hit.

I was still baffled on the timing of things. Piedmont and Poplar Buff were hit after Cairo. Perhaps it wasn't just one big toxic cloud but several.

Blocking out all of the disturbing noise, I sat at the table contemplating what I would do if the leads dried up at the airport. Chances were, they would.

My son was nearly eighteen. He made the decision to leave and not say anything.

It wasn't a matter of running into the next town and getting me a gift and getting trapped. He made a plan.

My heart broke because he wasn't with me. He wasn't close enough for me to protect. He was out there in a maddening world and there was nothing I could do.

"Hey," Perry spoke soft, pulling up a chair and joining me. "You have a second?"

"I have all the time until daylight."

"So, I was wondering if we can switch up." He grabbed the bottle and poured some brandy into his cup. "Trade up tomorrow."

"What do you mean, trade up?"

"Take PJ with you to the airport and I bring Martina with me to Charleston."

"Why?" I asked.

"I'm not sure what medical training she has, but she has some."

"She's a doctor," I said. "Well, she stopped practicing when she came to the mountain." I looked over at her. "I'm surprised she's not responding. How can she sleep?"

"She took a sleeping pill."

That shocked me. "How did she get one?"

"Guilty." He lifted his hand. "She saw me giving them out. No one got any rest yesterday; they need to sleep. Did you want one?"

"No. I have this." I lifted the cup. "Which I thank you for."

"Brandy is a calming booze. Anyhow, I went to hit the medical center, grab as much as that IV medicine, get stuff to run IV's and tranquilizers. Maybe a tranquilizer gun. At the very least they'll have one at the veterinarian."

"You're gonna try to save them."

Perry nodded. "*Try.* If I can sedate them enough. If they aren't too far gone. Like I said earlier, I read that case study. A man went in with lesions, they thought they were self-inflicted scratch marks and they put him in a psychiatric ward. He progressed negatively, despite treatment over seven days until he passed."

"If it was a case study, it wasn't this supped up version."

Perry shook his head. "But we're gonna give it a try. See what happens. I need her, and PJ can be a help to you."

"If she agrees, I'm fine with it. That's if my car is still in play," I said. "Someone was in it."

"Probably just moving it to that blockade they made. If not we'll find you a vehicle. You need to get to that airport to see."

"I saw your face when I mentioned what time his bus got here. You looked at PJ."

"I did," Perry replied. "We got the warning at 7:15. Which meant it arrived at 7:30. Maybe he took shelter somewhere. I mean, did he have a phone?"

I nodded. "He did."

"Then he got the warning. It went to every phone. If he is smart, he did what the warning said."

"I believe he is smart enough to get to shelter. I do. If he got that warning, he heeded it."

"Then he's still in town. If he's not at the airport, he's somewhere here. Maybe still hiding. We know folks survived it unscathed but aren't coming out."

"How do know he didn't leave?" I questioned.

"You think he was taking a plane, right?" Perry asked. "It's a quiet world, Lucy. I never heard a plane. Not saying it didn't happen, just saying I don't think any plane flew out of here. You have to check. You have to look. I know I would."

I hoped he was right. I hoped Vincent did find shelter and the buck stopped there in Cairo. All I wanted was to get my son and head back to Gideon.

Something in my gut told me it wasn't going to be that simple.

TWENTY-THREE

FINDING VINCENT

In my mind, I'd expected to emerge from the building into chaos and destruction, but outside the pharmacy building it was no more or less than when we went in.

With the exception of the pharmacy store front, the inside of the store was not too destroyed. Things had fallen, nothing deliberately busted. It sounded like it the night before, but they were just determined to find us and they didn't.

When Martina called Perry, 'Neville', I didn't know what she meant at first. Perry did and he wasn't that much older than me. She explained, how she likened it all to the movie Omega Man. I wasn't familiar with it, but once she explained it, I was more familiar with the remake.

In Omega Man, the creatures of the night retreated, they were more human looking and sick, and the man, Neville, in both versions, wanted to cure the sick and bring back the world.

She had agreed to go with Perry because she believed they had to try, if not for those people in Cairo but for those who probably hadn't gotten sick yet.

The spores were out there. They weren't dying off all that easy and we were all at risk.

Then again, I wasn't a medical person or scientist.

Martina and I were both scared to go out and find my car. Perry was right, they had only moved it to the barricade, and they didn't take anything from it.

Not only were they able to drive, they knew what they wanted.

Us.

Not to eat us like some wretched zombie film or suck our blood, it was to beat us to a pulp, take out their anger and kill us.

They remained with the psychosis.

My car had a weird smell when I got near it. A sour urine and vomit odor. Before I even got inside, Martina stopped me, she always had her bag over her shoulder and from it she pulled out wipes from a plastic bag. They were wet and she proceeded to wipe off the steering wheel and seats.

"Give it a second to dry," she told me.

I could smell the alcohol from the homemade wipes. A few seconds later, I got in the car, started it and immediately reached for the radio.

We both needed to be sure home was fine. I wasn't sure how it even missed us, if it did.

Al replied instantly. "Lucy, are you guys okay?! We lost contact with you."

"Fine. Everything okay there?"

"Roger that. Your girl was worried."

"Tell her not to be. We're fine. It's too detailed to say what happened, but know, some kind of weapon hit down here and people are sick. I'm gonna follow the trail and see if I can find Vincent while Martina helps a man here with the sick."

"What kind of sickness?" Al asked.

"Ever see the movie *The Crazies*?"

"Are you serious?" he asked.

"Sort of. We'll check in soon, I promise."

"Let us know about Vincent. And make sure you check in. Avery would like to speak with you. She is with Mr. Parson now at the hen house."

After ending the radio call, I thought about how I conveyed it to him. I wasn't sure any pop culture reference would work. As far as I knew Al had been in Gideon a long time.

He seemed to have gotten the gist of what I was saying. In reality it wasn't far off.

After moving the car from the barricade, I checked the gas. I had enough to get back home so I gave one of the cans I had in the back to Perry, wished him and Martina well and took off with PJ.

"How long to the airport?" I asked as we left the block.

"Ten minutes tops," he replied.

"Have you lived here your entire life?"

PJ shook his head. "Not my entire life. Most though. When we moved here, it was a ghost town. Now it still looks it. My grandmother lived here and my dad wanted to be close to her and my aunt. My mom passed when I was three. Anyhow, Dad was a pharmacist and the nearest one was in Charleston, so he bought the store and reopened the old pharmacy here, made it sort of a mom-and-pop grocery. When they rebuilt the river ports, we really thought things would boom again."

"It didn't?"

"Just a little. Not as much as folks hoped. I'd hear stories about how this place was gleaming, but no one is here. Those who stayed, stayed because it was cheap and nowhere else to go. Like my gram."

We talked that short trip. He was a polite young man and I joked that I didn't hold it against him for his alien theory.

He just started his second year of college. I was glad I was getting to know the man responsible for saving my life.

The airport was nowhere near what I expected it to be. I really envisioned some sort of little hut in the middle of the airfield. Not massive like one would see at a major international perhaps a few hangers. I was surprised when not only was there a couple small hangers, a larger one, and a building that looked like a small version of a big terminal. It actually looked fairly new. Glass front windows, an archway over the front entrance that would match any you would see in front of a Holiday Inn.

"Is that it?" PJ asked as we stopped the car.

"What? The airport? I would assume so."

"No. That plane." He pointed to the small private jet on the side of the one hanger.

"Maybe it belongs to someone in the area."

PJ laughed hysterically, then drew serious. "No. It landed here. It's parked, not in a hanger and the door is open with the stairs."

"Let's go check it out." I opened my car door, taking my keys with me. Even though it was daylight, I wasn't taking a chance.

With a blip-blip of my key fob, I locked the doors and walked toward the plane. A few steps into my walk, I came to a halt. "Forgot the rifle."

"We're good." PJ patted the waist, indicating to a revolver. "Plus, if we run into any..." He peered to the sky. "It's bright. They won't chase us out here."

"Are you sure?"

"Oh, yeah. Yesterday afternoon," PJ explained, "I ran into Doug, he was cool and calm and then snapped. When he came for me, I ran out. He was in the street a second before he screamed and ran back in. Like we said, the light hurts their sores."

I looked ahead to the plane. It was a good hundred yards from us, appearing as if it taxied off the small runway.

As we neared it, I saw the open door and expected the smell of death to hit is as we got closer. Finding bodies was not a shock anymore, it was the norm.

Approaching the stairs, there was a smell. But not of death this time. It was a mixture of coffee, booze and something sweet, I couldn't place.

Being chivalrous, PJ insisted he'd go first. After he boarded, he called out to me to join him. I walked up the steps and entered the plane.

It was a beautiful small plane with limited head room.

A couch style bench seat was against one side, and two bucket seats and small table on the other side of the plane. On the table was a cup and plate. Half-eaten toast and it looked like coffee. There was a blanket and pillow on the couch, and perched on the tiny table at the end was an empty wine glass.

I looked to my right, the sliding door for the cockpit was partially open.

That's where I expected the body, but it was empty.

When I turned around, PJ was standing at the table with this hand on the cup. "It's still warm. Whoever is alive was here not long ago."

"We didn't see anyone. Where could they be?"

"Let's check the hangers and the main terminal."

A part of me thought we should just call out, 'Hello, is anyone here,' but after the previous night's run in, I wasn't taking that chance.

"How did they survive?" I asked. "I mean they were here last night, someone slept in there."

"Maybe they arrived after or flew above the cloud if that's possible."

The first hanger we passed the doors were open. PJ looked, no one was inside. There was a small twin engine plane in there, but no bodies or people.

While I didn't see a body as we approached the main building, I could smell the rotting flesh when the winds blew.

"There's a body out here somewhere," said PJ. "Not surprising, this is a busy airport for cargo, despite how small the town is."

"And according to your dad, other things too."

"Eh." PJ waved out his hand. "That's an old story that goes around."

"It's a well-known story then. Mr. Parson from our community said it." I stopped before the door. "Ready?"

PJ looked through the glass. "Seems empty."

In an unusual turn of events, the second I opened the door I smelled Pine Sol or something like it.

A fresh smell, almost too strong. It was odd.

Stepping in, not only did the outside look like a hotel, but the inside did as well. A small lobby type with vending machines and a couple tables. A counter desk to the right. Two closed doors behind the counter, which I assumed were offices.

It was bright in there, loads of natural light came through the floor to ceiling length windows.

"Looks empty," said PJ. "Smells like someone just cleaned." He looked down, then crouched before a table.

"What is it?"

"Blood." He lifted his fingers, then wiped them on his leg. "Not a lot but still blood."

"Oh, PJ, go wash your hands or something, please." I shuddered at how nonchalant he was.

"The blood is fresh." He pulled out his revolver and looked around. He walked behind the counter and I followed.

"I don't think anyone is here," I said. "Honestly. Maybe whoever was on that plane eating toast cut themselves?"

"Or maybe whoever was on that plane is dead."

"Was there enough blood for that?" I asked. Behind the counter area was small. It didn't look touched. Or messy. I peered down to the counter and to the computer and a clipboard of papers. "Hey there's a computer and stuff, maybe we can find out who owns that plane and when it landed."

I reached for the clipboard and it toppled from my hand when the slightly muffled voice called out.

"Mom? Mom? Is that you?"

I spun around. "Vincent!"

"Mom! In here."

I shifted my eyes looking for where he called from.

"There." PJ pointed to the left office door.

It was my son, my heart pounded so fast as I pushed passed PJ and reached for the knob. It was locked. "It's locked, can you open it."

"No," Vincent replied. "I can't."

I faced PJ. "See if you can find a key."

He nodded and rushed over to the counter.

"Vincent are you okay? I am so glad you're okay."

"Found keys," PJ said, jingling them.

He handed me the ring with four keys. The first two didn't fit, but the third slid right it. "Got it."

"Stop!" a woman's voice hollered. "Please. Don't open that door."

TWENTY-FOUR

KEPT IN THE DARK

Sonya was as shocked to see me as I was to see her.

"Mrs. Carver, please, don't open that door," she begged. "Take out the key."

I hadn't moved, but PJ, placed his hand over mine and removed the key.

"What are you doing?" I snapped.

"Look at her. If she is telling you not to open it. I wouldn't open it."

Finally, I really looked at Sonya as she stepped closer.

Her hair was pulled in a ponytail, the glamor actress wore no makeup. A huge scratch ran down the side of her face and her left eye was not only bruised under, but the white was deep red. She extended her bandaged hand to PJ for the key.

He gave it to her.

"Thank you," she said.

"Was that your blood on the table?" PJ asked.

"Yeah, I ran to get the first aid kit. I broke a glass." She lifted her hand. "It's been a rough morning."

Slightly irritated, lifted my hand. "I'm sorry you're hurt, but again, why can't I open that door for my son?"

"Because he's sick. Something is wrong with him. He's not in his right mind, he may sound it now," Sonya said. "But he'll switch up. Trust me.'

"Does he have the sores?" PJ asked.

Sonya nodded.

"But you're fine," PJ said.

"And so is Brian the pilot. He moved a few more bodies out of here. We were cleaning up."

I faced the door, laying my hand on it. "Vincent. Hey. Listen, we're going to get you help."

"Who's there?" Vincent asked.

"Mom."

"You're not my mother. You're one of them," Vincent replied.

"Them," Sonya said. "He's not seeing us right. He just attacks."

Stepping away from the door, I rubbed my arm and paced. "PJ, we have to figure out how to get him sedated and out of there and back to town."

"Or," PJ proposed, "bring the help here."

"You open that door," Sonya said. "You don't know what you'll face. When we opened it last night, thinking he was better, it was nearly impossible to get him back in. Not without injury anyway. It's safer for him and for everybody."

"And what?" I asked. "Leave him in there to die? To starve? I'll get him out of there."

"You'll get hurt," Sonya said.

"And do you think I care if I get injured?" I asked. "That's my son. And why is he here? Huh? Why?"

"Lucy," PJ gave a soft warning.

"No. I want to know." I looked at her. "Why is my son in this godforsaken town? When he could be up at Gideon, safe and sound."

"Because he didn't want to be there anymore. I told him, I would get him. At first I told him to wait it out. I was going to the bunker and I'd contact him. Then he called and said he was on his way to get a bus to Nashville. Brian said we could get him here in Cairo if he could make it. He was already off the mountain. So, I did my best."

"Well, your best isn't good enough. He's sick," I snapped. "Did he know what was happening? Because this shit started days ago."

"He didn't know it all. I just told him things were bad. I was vague. No one really understood what was happening. So, it was hard to explain."

"How did you not get sick?" I asked.

"Luck. Maybe. It wasn't supposed to be here as early as it was," Sonya defended. "When Vincent told me he had left the mountain, my concern was to get him out of Piedmont and whatever that Bluff town is, because the expert in the bunker said it was hitting there at night. So why would we think it would hit Cairo first?"

"Well, we didn't have an expert telling us anything. My son walked right into it."

"Lucy," PJ spoke calmly. "Listen, as shitty as this situation is, what's done is done. We can't change what happened. We can only deal with what is in front of us and that is Vincent."

"I know. But I'm angry. I am so angry right now. Angry that none of this would have happened if she didn't give them the phone and string him along. I'm angry because my son knew things were happening down here and he said nothing."

"He wanted you safe," Sonya said. "He knew you guys were safe."

"Stop! Just stop!" I blasted. "You manipulated him. He's seventeen years old. Now he is sick, losing his mind and possibly dying and that…" I pointed towards the locked door. "Is on you."

At the end of my words, with what sounded like a sob, Sonya turned and rushed away.

"Okay, see now," PJ said. "You made her cry."

"Oh, like I care." I faced the door again. "I only care right now about helping my son." I shifted my eyes to PJ. "How do we get in there to do that?"

"You found him?" Avery asked with such glee in her voice. "Mommy, I knew you would."

"Baby, he's sick. Remember what we saw in Piedmont? The dead police officer? That's one version. The other version of the sickness is a slow burn. It doesn't kill you, it rides you out."

"Is Vincent gonna die?"

"Not if I can do anything about it," I replied. "Martina and a man named Perry think they may be able to help people. I'm with Vincent now. I'll know more tomorrow. I just wanted you to know I was okay."

"I love you."

"I love you too sweetie."

We chatted a few more minutes. Avery told me about the good food Al's wife made, but she missed our cabin. I told her she was able to go back whenever she wanted as long as she checked in daily with someone.

Our cabin.

After I ended the conversation, I thought about what Sonya told me. How Vincent seemed fine when they arrived, but in the course of an hour he developed the sores, fever chills. By morning the sun hurt him so badly they moved him into the office. She believed the sunlight was causing his horrid moods, but soon realized it was the sickness.

I sat in my car outside the main terminal thinking about how things may have been if Vincent just waited one more day. One more day before racing after Sonya. One more day and everything would have been fine. More than likely, we wouldn't have known anything for a while.

Bodies would have rotted by the time Jeff made his monthly trip. None of the crazies would have been seen. Just a quiet world. One we no longer needed to get away from or off the grid because things would have been reset.

It was a strange thought process mainly because I didn't long for civilization. I wasn't going to mourn the loss of technology. I hadn't used it really in months and didn't miss it.

Even before we moved to Gideon, my phone was mainly for talking to my husband and keeping in touch with my kids. Outside of my work, I didn't have social life. I got to a certain point in my life I didn't need one. I had my family.

There was nothing, absolutely nothing other than the occasional Starbucks that I missed about the world I left behind.

But just two days out of Gideon and I was missing the cabin. The warmth of it, the simplicity of life on the mountain.

Now I sat at an airport in the middle of the stinking world I left behind, while my son was locked in an office for everyone's safety.

I felt guilty sitting in the car while he was in that office. The mother in me felt as if I needed to be outside that door.

I had to wait. PJ and Sonya took a truck and were headed back toward town to find Martina and Perry. If they needed to test their cure, then Vincent was a prime candidate.

Knowing I'd head back in, I reached for the radio, maybe scan to see if anyone else was on the airwaves, when I saw the pilot walking from the plane.

I assumed it was the pilot. I hadn't met him at all. From a distance it didn't look like he was sick. He wore a white tee shirt and dress pants, and he carried something in his hands. A taller, fit man that walked focused from that plane, never noticing me in the car like some sort of stalker.

When I saw him go into the terminal, I was fearful. Immediately, I panicked with an unprovoked neuroticism that he was going in there to kill my son.

I don't know why I thought that or why it even crossed my mind.

Thoughts of this guy waiting for Sonya to leave, getting rid of the sick, rabid child.

Hurriedly, I jumped from the car and at a fast pace, walked to the terminal. I thought about how I would defend him. How I would stop him. Nearly, at the door, I stopped, turned around, went back to the car and retrieved my rifle.

Again, there was no rhyme or reason for me to think that this pilot, Brian, was killing my son. I just had an unnatural fear of it.

Making sure, the gun was loaded, I walked into the terminal. Sure enough, he was standing by the office door, listening.

I raised my rifle.

He turned some, saw me, and gave this look I wasn't expecting. A scrunched up facial expression, lifting his hands as if to convey, 'what's going on?'

I held aim.

The he widened his eyes, annoyed and mouthed the words, "What the fuck?"

As soon as I opened my mouth to speak, he put his finger to his mouth to make me be quiet, then showed me the finger, telling me to hold on.

My arms were aching holding that gun. I wished he'd give me a reason to shoot or not.

He pointed to a small, shoe size box on the counter, lowering the rifle, I walked over.

In it was a bottle of water, crackers, a mini box of corn flakes and a little Hostess cake.

Not moving his stance, Brian huffed out, then reached for the box.

I got it. He was wanting me to get it for him.

Again, he listened to the door, and oh so slowly inserted the key.

I watched as he moved as if any noise would detonate a land mine. In an essence it could.

He turned the key, cringed when he thought he made a noise, then waited.

When Vincent didn't make a sound, Brian crouched down. While close to the floor, he set down the box, then reached up and turned the knob.

He inched the door open, silently and enough to push the box through. Once it was in, he hurriedly stood and pulled the door closed.

Immediately, I heard Vincent screaming and growling, much like he did when he threw temper tantrums as a child.

He banged from the other side of the door, causing it to rattle. A short-lived battle over that doorknob ensued until Brian finally locked it again.

I was in shock. Listening to Vincent bang on the door, screaming in a maddening way to let him out.

Brian exhaled in relief.

I felt ashamed. I was ready to kill a man whose only crime was trying to feed my child.

My first interaction with Brian wasn't smooth.

He was angry as he stepped away from the counter and walked to the vending area.

"What the hell, lady?!" he shouted. "Why did you aim that gun on me? World is over and you're coming to an airport to shoot people. What could I possibly have that you want? You want me to fly you somewhere? Forget it."

"I'm his mother."

"What? Whose?"

"Vincent's."

He laughed a single, sarcastic, 'ha' and shook his head. "Let me get this straight. You're his mom and you're aiming at me to kill me when I am trying to get him food so he doesn't die."

"I thought you were trying to kill him."

"Why would I do that?" he asked.

"Because he's…he's…"

"He's sick. End of story. He can't get well if he starves to death." Brain reached to his back pocket and pulled out a small airline size bottle of booze. After uncapping it, he downed it.

"You know it's like only ten in the morning, right?"

"What are you the new prohibition?" He placed the empty bottle on a table and sat down, rubbing his eyes.

"I'm sorry," I apologized and walked over to him. "My name is Lucy." I extended my hand.

He slid his fingers down the bridge of his nose and raised his eyes to my hand.

I held it there, waiting.

"Brian." He shook it without enthusiasm.

"Brian, I am sorry." I sat down with him. "I don't know what I was thinking. I just got scared. My mind just took off. Like you were waiting for Sonya to leave."

"And I would kill him?" Brian shook his head. "Sonya told me she was leaving to find help. That the young man with her had a means."

I nodded. "In a way, yeah."

"She failed to tell me Vincent's mother was here."

"Sonya fails to tell people a lot of things," I said. "Like telling my son a killer cloud was rolling across the world, killing people. If she did, Vincent would have stayed behind."

"From what I gathered, Vincent wasn't happy up on that mountain. Not that it's a reason to aid a runaway, but he was already off the mountain. And what are you talking about, killer cloud. Is that what you people on the mountain think?"

"No, I didn't even know about it. It was all a surprise when I came to find Vincent."

"Wow," he said. "That's a hell of a thing to walk into."

"Tell me about it," I replied. "I wasn't expecting it."

"It's not a cloud. Where did you hear that?" He paused and nodded. "Television? Radio? Media?"

"No, actually," I stated. "From a pharmacist named Perry. He said he got an alert it was arriving. They were told to get below ground."

Brian nodded. "Or above."

"The toxic fog or something was rolling through."

Brian laughed.

"What? What is so funny?"

"Do you hear yourself? A toxic cloud or fog that retains strength?"

"Well, it's a weapon, it has to be," I said. "With a hell of a delivery system."

"It's a weapon alright." Brian stood. "It's not a cloud. Come on."

"Where are you going?" I asked.

"Taking you," he said. "To learn the truth."

TWENTY-FIVE

OVERHEARD

What would the world become?

Would be a wasteland full of Mad Maxx wannabes with a blatant disregard for morality, rules and decency? Or would mankind rise above the petty nature and become responsible for each other, help each other.

I didn't know. No one did. Only time would tell.

The voices on the plane's radio carried on across every channel Brian searched.

There were people out there that survived, and were planning what to do next. People looking for answers, with others giving information that they had. Some looking for others, some protecting what was theirs and I assumed, others that were just listening, so they knew where to go to get what they needed.

To know such a massive deadly event occurred and so many survived just scared the hell out of me.

The electricity was still on.

The water still pumped through the pipes and cell phones worked.

But for how long?

Once those modern conveniences were done with, I imagined a desperate world.

One I didn't want to be a part of. I knew once my son was better, if that happened, I was taking my family and running again for the hills. Only this time, better prepared than when we first arrived.

But really? How safe was that?

How long would we be safe guarded from the desperate world below us?

I had no idea, when I followed Brian, what he was going to show me or tell me. He took me to the tiny cockpit. Small airline bottles of booze were scattered about the floor; he kicked them clear and sat down.

"This is the world," he said and reached for the radio.

I listened to the voices, the desperation, the anger of each person as he perused the channels like Ted used to do with the radio in the car.

"Anyone know if it's still out there?"

"Burgettstown here, we need water. Our water is out."

"Sam's Club Warehouse in West Mifflin is not safe."

"I have marks on my hand. Why am I getting these sores? This happened three days ago."

"Is the government still running?"

"No one knows for sure what will happen next," Brian said. "We do know what has happened. Maybe they ..." He pointed to the radio. "Don't, but people like Sonya, the privileged, they do."

"What do you mean?"

"Private channel." He changed the radio.

It came in mid broadcast. It was the weather I believed. Then the man started talking like a professional radio host. Maybe he was.

"For those of you turning in, not yet here," the voice on the radio said. "No reports of the illness in the bunker. We hope you get here soon. The president is waiting four more days before he makes an official statement to the public. Kinda waiting for things to die down. No pun intended."

"What the hell?" I asked. "Who is this asshole?"

"Mark Monroe."

"The Talk Show host?" I asked.

Brian nodded. "He's in the celebrity bunker."

"What is that?"

"Well, it's not just celebrities, it's politicians, athletes. Basically, people that can afford to buy their way in," Brian replied. "But they have been paying their dues for a long time."

"Where's it at?" I asked.

"Kentucky. We were going to pick up your boy and head there," Brian replied. "But when we arrived, he started getting the sores on his hands and face. He hadn't lost his way yet, if you know what I mean. But by nightfall he was talking crazy shit and the next day he attacked Sonya."

"You could have left him. I appreciate that you didn't."

"Don't give me any credit," Brian said. "I wanted to leave but Sonya felt she needed to stay. She was worried about Vincent."

"Yet, you didn't fly off."

Brian shook his head. "Nah, I stayed. I mean, I don't know her all that well, but from what I was hearing, there weren't many of us left unaffected. Which doesn't mean we won't get it. And to be honest, I wanted in that bunker. Abandoning her was not the way to do it."

"She's not here. You still took food to my son," I said.

"He's a kid. I'm gonna do what I can."

"Thank you." I exhaled. "I appreciate that."

"Do you think they can cure him?" Brian asked.

"I hope, but I don't know. What I do know is, if we can cure him, we can cure others. The trick is getting them to take the treatment."

"Whatever this is, it really hits the brain."

"It's a fungus."

"You don't say." Brian nodded. "No wonder you guys think you can cure it."

"*Hope* we can cure it," I corrected. "Brian, you said, you were going to tell me the truth. What is it? What do you know?"

"I brought you here to listen to the radio so you know I am picking things up," he said. "There are people in the bunker that are experts, are studying it."

Awfully convenient that they were already there."

"They weren't. Once this started, the people registered with the bunker grabbed any expert they could. And they give the best answers they could. I didn't hear it was a fungus."

"What did you hear it was?" I asked.

"Virus. But they weren't exposed or testing anyone, so I'll tell them what you've told me. But I can tell you this. It didn't carry in a cloud."

"So, it wasn't a weapon?"

"Oh, it was a weapon," Brian said. "Who sent it still remains a mystery."

"PJ," I said. "The young man with me, thinks it was aliens. Have you heard anything about that?"

"There's speculation. But if it is aliens, why would they use one of the oldest means of transportation as a delivery system."

"What do you mean?" I asked.

"Everyone thinks biological weapon. They think bomb, or something right. No one thinks about it being delivered across the country by way of smoke. Lucy, the reason people think it was a cloud was because it was ejected into the air as a form of steam."

"How?" I asked.

"Trains. That's what the experts are saying in the bunker. It was carried west to east, north to south, by way of train car. One day. One pay load. Everyone dies. Look, I went to the library yesterday and found this." He pulled forward a book and opened it. It was of the US and lines ran all over it. "These are railways. Look how many."

"Is it just here?"

Brian shrugged. "I don't know. We haven't had contact with anyone outside the US in days. But even if it just happened here, the effects around the world will be devastating."

"Any theories from the super bunker about who did this?"

"Theories are abound," he replied. "But does it matter? I mean, it happened right? Now all we can do is move on and reverse the damage if it can be done."

The key word was 'if'. With my entire soul and being, I hoped for my son's sake it could be reversed.

TWENTY-SIX

RELEASE

My glimmer of hope started to flicker and dim with every hour that passed. PJ and Sonya had not returned and I was concerned. Worried more so for Perry and Martina because they went to the other town to get what they needed.

It had been a couple of days, people were bound to be emerging from their hideouts. I was fearful that they ran into trouble.

Vincent reminded me of my father with Alzheimer's. Good moments, then bad. Lucid, not lucid. Fits of anger and delusion. The fungus definitely reached the brain. Was so much damaged caused that it would be hard to turn back?

I tried several times talking to him. Telling him stories of his youth, how he was on the mountain, why he left. I talked about his favorite foods, books, even his trading cards.

In fleeting, short spurts, he'd have moments where he understood what was happening, where he knew he was sick and he knew who I was. But just as fast as he was lucid, in a snap of a finger he was not.

He didn't trust us, and he threw raging fits, slamming his body against the door, while screaming obscenities at me.

I had to remind myself that it was the sickness talking, not my son.

But I worried. I worried what kind of damage he was doing to himself. With all the banging and pounding, surely, he was injured.

He was a learning tool, as well. If Vincent had moments of reason, those in Cairo and anywhere else had them as well.

Would we wait for the moment of reason to come before getting him to agree to treatment? They lasted too short to get a sentence out, which left me to wonder, when PJ returned with Martina or Perry, just how would we get to Vincent? And how would we administer a cure safely for everyone else.

Those thoughts would have to wait, because it all depended on whether or not we were even able to get the medication.

I hadn't eaten all day and I think Brian knew that. He was actually a really nice guy, nicer than I initially gave him credit for.

He persuaded me away from my seat on the floor, by the locked office, with food. Brian wasn't taking 'no' for an answer.

"Forgive me for not doing the proper presentation," he said setting down two little trays on the table. One for him and one for me. They reminded me of the old style TV dinners with the sections and all. "Usually, we have a flight attendant put it on a plate to make it presentable. Take it out of the little sections."

"I don't need all that."

"Good. Neither do I. I didn't grab the salad, unless you want one." He sat down.

"No, this is great."

"Wine."

"Please." As he poured, I examined my food tray. I knew one thing was asparagus, and there were potatoes in the other compartment. I wasn't sure what the pastry looking thing was. I adjusted the tray. "This looks amazing."

"You should see it on the fine china."

"Okay, what is this?" I pointed to the pastry. "It smells wonderful."

"Because it is. That is beef Wellington."

"I have never had it."

"Wait until you try it. Just cut into it. One thing about Sonya is, she always has the best food. Really. It gets made by a chef and we put it in the little oven on the plane. Of course, the Citation galley is small."

"Citation?"

"Cessna Citation, that's the plane out there."

With an 'ah,' I nodded. "Is it yours?"

"No. No." He shook his head. "I work for a company. Typically, Sonya gets bigger planes. Her plane is bigger, but it wasn't ready. This was. One of the people in the bunker had it and offered it."

"And yet." I cut into my beef pastry. "She still managed to have gourmet meals."

"I don't think she can take full credit. The world was kinda nuts when she took off and the food was already on board."

"And you?'

"I was in the bunker," he replied. "Our whole company team was for when, you know, people emerged. I offered to go."

As I plunged my fork into the Wellington, I glanced down. "Holy crap this is a steak in here."

"Yep. Probably more well done than it should be," he said. "But given it had to be heated. It's forgivable."

I took a bite. "Oh my God, this is amazing. Are these mushrooms."

He nodded as he smiled. "Eat up. Unless you're down there in that bunker, who knows when you'll eat like this again, right?"

"I have never eaten like this. So, I take it there aren't any more prepared gourmet meals left?"

"There are."

"Thank you for this," I said. "Thank you very much."

"You needed to step away from the door."

"I needed to step away. Period." I lifted my glass and took a drink. "I feel guilty eating this."

"Don't. If someone doesn't eat it, it will go to waste."

"So, are you going back to the bunker?"

"I don't know," he said. "It's a different world out here. There is no status. No rich and famous, no poor. Like a do-over, everyone is the same. One..." He pointed as he lifted his glass. "I think some are better prepared to handle all this more than others. Like you."

"No." I shook my head.

"You were living off grid."

"Doesn't mean I know how to survive," I said. "I ran away to that community. Ran away from all the pain, all the media, all the crap. I wasn't ready. In fact, Sonya made it as convenient as possible for us in that cabin. A solar generator so we always had power. It was completely stocked with food. Not like this, but still. My Ma and Pa Kettle skills were not put to work. Not yet."

"I'm going to be very honest with you. I don't know your story. All I know is a very panicked Sonya Haze was running around looking for a pilot so she could save her friend. I volunteered"

"She didn't tell you anything?" I asked.

"Only that he was living semi off grid. They kept in touch and he had left the safety of the community. She was frantic, Lucy, I mean really frantic. He wasn't answering and he hadn't a clue what he was walking into."

"Why didn't she tell him?" I asked.

"I questioned her on that. Why she was never straight forward with him about the bio weapon."

"And?"

"And she never thought he'd leave you," Brian said. "She never thought he would leave the community especially after she told him things were bad. When she told me that I told her, that wasn't how teenage minds work."

"I'm not sure how they work. It's been quite a few years for me."

"Me as well. Just so you know, from what she told me, she didn't encourage him to leave. She encouraged him to stay where he was."

I took a long sip of my wine and waited a moment to have more food, then I asked. "Why? Did you ask her why she wanted a teenage boy? I mean, she is so much older. Why the interest? She's in her thirties."

"No, she's not. She looks it," Brian stated and took a bite of his food. "She's young. Media says she is thirty something. I've seen her without make up. She's a puppy."

"I didn't notice how young or old she looked," I stated. "I just knew some…cougar, for lack of better word, was after my child."

"From what I hear in a couple weeks he's eighteen."

"From what I hear," I said. "The term is called grooming."

Brian was serious for a moment, then he laughed as if I were telling the funniest joke. Maybe it was just the tension of the events.

We finished our meal, putting the conversation of Sonya to the side, while drinking that really good wine. He didn't have much story to tell other than he wasn't married, but was engaged until she broke it off because of his job. He was in the air force before becoming a private pilot.

That was it.

Just as we completed talking about that and moved on to the topic of baseball, I heard the door.

Instantly, my heart dropped to my stomach. Especially when Brian abruptly stood.

Something was wrong.

I was scared for a moment that it was something bad. By the time I stood up, slightly lightheaded from the wine, I saw PJ, Sonya, and Martina walk in.

"We got the stuff," Martina lifted a bag. "Where's your son?"

Gasping out in relief, I lifted my hand gesturing for them to give me a moment. Heart racing out of control, I reached behind me, lifted my glass and finished off my wine in one long gulp.

Martina set down a box on the front counter desk. She looked exhausted. Her hair was a bit unruly and she had dark circles under her eyes.

"I am so glad that you are okay," I said with exasperation laced relief. "All of you. I was worried."

"It wasn't easy," Martina replied. "Perry and I had some difficulty finding what we needed in bulk. We can't just help one, that was our train of thought. Imagine my surprise when we got back to Cairo and I saw PJ."

"We waited for them," PJ stated. "I didn't think it was a good idea to chase them."

"And also," Martina added. "Imagine my happiness to find out Vincent was alive. Lucy, I am so happy." She reached over and grabbed my arm. "You did it. You found him. You were so determined. That is a mother's love. We are gonna do all that we can. Okay?"

"Will it work?" I asked.

"We can hope and give it our best shot," said Martina. "Remember there is a chance it won't work."

"I know," I said.

"If it does, we aren't just helping Vincent. We're on the path to helping others. After we get Vincent started and know that it works, then we'll try to figure out a way to do the same for others. Sonya said there's a bunker."

Sonya spoke up. "I am not sure how many will do it, but when this works on Vincent, I want to get as many people involved as I can to help those inflicted."

"That's a lot of sick people," I said.

"Let's not think that far ahead," Martina said. "One step at a time. Right now, Vincent. Okay?"

"Okay." I nodded.

"Now." Martina tapped the box. "I have good news and bad news."

"Oh, boy," I said. "What is it?"

"The good news is we got everything we think we need to try to cure him, including the tranquilizer and some sedation. The bad news is we don't have a tranquilizer gun, so we are gonna have to be hands on to do it."

So, there we were, ready to go but the holdup was a big one.

Martina continued, "We need to figure out how to get to Vincent in a way that is safe for everyone including him."

"We discussed this in the truck," Perry said.

Brian asked, "What did you discuss? What did you come up with?"

"We thought about going in there." Perry pointed.

Brian laughed sarcastically. "No. No, it's small and dark and no room for defense."

Sonya said, "We could just open the door, but this..." She pointed up. "Is too bright. We know it burns them."

"We can't have him get any worse," Martina stated. "If those sores get inflamed, they can kill him as well."

"So, what do we do?" I asked.

Martina shifted her eyes about. "I say we wait. We take the far corner of the waiting area, get it set up for him. Get the IV ready and wait for dark."

"So, turn off all the lights," I said. "Open the door and try to catch him. Without getting hurt." I faced Brian. "How bad is he?"

"He's not dumb, Lucy," Brian replied. "He's smart. The sickness just seemed to enhance it. Look at Sonya. She opened the door, what, an inch or so to slip in his food, he blasted out of there, grabbed her, started beating on her and it took everything I had to pull him away. Then I…I had to hit him in the head just to slow him down enough to put him back in the office."

"We're sorry," Sonya said. "No one meant to hurt him."

I lifted my hand. "I understand. I do and this is all knowledge we need. So, let's take this time, right now, before the sun goes down," I said. "And come up with a plan."

TWENTY-SEVEN

DASH

Brian suggested that if we were going to openly speak about a plan, then we needed to do it outside and away from earshot of Vincent.

"He's listening," Brian said. "I'm convinced of it."

Outside of the terminal, we did just that.

We devised a simple plan.

After we set up the treatment area for Vincent, once night had come, we'd turn off all lights in the terminal and open the door.

Then the plan went into effect.

Admittedly, it was really simple.

Open door, get Vincent, sedate him.

"Alright, Martina," Brian said. "You will be out of sight and safe with that syringe. PJ and I will stand to the side of the door. Sonya you'll stand away from the counter in his view. He'll see you and come for you. PJ and I will tackle him from behind. Be fast, come for him, and don't hesitate."

"Got it." Martina nodded.

"How long will it take?" Brian asked.

"It will take a minute," she replied.

"Wait." I lifted my hand. "Back up. You want to use Sonya as bait?"

Brian nodded. "I think it's best."

"And what do I do?" I asked.

"Stay with Martina," he replied.

"No." I shook my head. "He is my son. If anyone is going to be bait it is going to be me."

Just as adamant as I was, Brian was as well. "No," he said. "You can get hurt."

"Better me than her." I pointed. "Do you think she can physically take it better than me?"

"It has nothing to do with that," Brian said. "It has everything to do with him being your son. He knows and how he behaves isn't going to mysteriously leave his mind. I hope it does, but we can't count on it. The boy has already been through so much, do we really want him to carry the guilt of attacking his mother? And what if…what if he kills you? He kills you, we cure him, how does he deal with that?"

"It's not going to happen," I said. "I'll stand at a distance. I'll be the bait. No arguments and I'll put my trust in you and PJ to get him."

We went back and forth for a little more until I finally won the argument, and Brian relented with a disgruntled. "Fine."

It didn't take too long to set up the treatment area. It did, however, seem like an eternity waiting for the sun to go down and for it to get dark.

I was a bit anxious. Watching the sky wasn't going to make it dark any faster. I was never one for patiently waiting.

Once it did get dark, and we shut off all the lights in the small terminal. It was scary. I finished off another glass of that wine to ease my nerves. I knew if I didn't, I would start to shake and feel that 'gut trembling' nervousness.

PJ said from what he knew we had one minute. If Vincent was quiet and calm, he would turn, but he would process the situation around him before he went violent.

The calm lasted sixty second give or take.

Martina was out of sight and closer to the treatment area.

I was on the other side of the counter in plain view of that office door.

PJ was on one side, Brian on the other and Sonya, I believed was, out of Vincent's peripheral and in the area of the vending lounge.

Waiting and waiting.

Staring at the closed office door waiting for the moment they would open it.

At first it was so dark, that I could barely see.

Then my eyes adjusted enough that I could see PJ and Brian.

I nodded that I was ready.

None of us made a sound or said a word.

Slowly and quietly, Brian unlocked the door, stepped back to the side and opened it.

He turned the knob and gave it a slight nudge to open it a mere inch then he left it be.

Waiting for Vincent.

Once he stepped out, they would get him, Martina would sedate him and we'd get him started on the treatment.

It seemed to take forever for Vincent to appear. I worried that he was worse, that maybe even that he passed.

My heart ached even thinking of that.

It took a while, then finally, the door flung open.

Vincent stood in the doorway and I was able to see him. Even though dark, I could see my son.

He was pale and covered with those sores. It broke my heart to see him so fragile and ill. He immediately locked eyes with me.

"Mom?" he whimpered out. "Mom, I'm so sick."

"Baby, I know. I know. I'm right here." I heard it in his voice, my son, he wasn't some madman. Not yet.

I knew they were ready for him, ready to grab him. For a second I wondered if it was going to be easier than we thought.

"Vincent." I took a step. "Listen, I can help you get better. There's medicine."

"Mom."

"Yes."

"Mom"

"What is it?"

Then as if my son left the body of the boy before me, he blasted. "You can't lie to me! You're not my mother! They…" He swung to his right and his flailing arm nailed PJ.

PJ jolted back falling to the floor.

As Brian stepped into Vincent, my son, grabbed him, and careened his own head into Brian's and Brian stumbled back.

It all happened so fast.

Like some amped up, steroid induced wrestler, he clenched his fist and growled, "I see you! You can't get me."

With a single step and a leap that I didn't know was humanly possible, he jumped on the counter. In a slightly crouched positioned, he looked at me.

I was ready.

I waited.

But his sights went elsewhere and he jumped back off the counter.

I knew it, he saw Sonya.

Brian and PJ finally got their footing. I could tell they knew at the same moment as I did what Vincent was going to do.

They moved for him, but my son was too fast. She didn't move. Sonya just stood there, scared and frozen.

Vincent raged across the terminal toward Sonya, something inside of me kicked in, adrenaline like I never felt, pulsed through my veins and I raced after my son.

I knew by how he looked and how he moved, that if he got ahold of Sonya, there would be no pulling him away. I had to stop him. I didn't know how I had the strength, but as his hand reached out to her and she screamed, I forged ahead, throwing everything I had into stopping him.

It was the perfect interception even though I physically felt it.

Lunging forward, shoulder first, still running full speed, I rammed into Vincent. I threw all of my momentum and weight into that hit. The flowing adrenaline did nothing to halt me from feeling the intense pain as my shoulder connected with his rib cage.

The force of my run and hit was enough to not only stop him from getting Sonya, but it knocked him back and down to the floor.

Vincent fell on his side and I landed on top of him. In a sense we were both still moving and together we ended up in a slide across the floor.

The moment our slide ceased, without missing a beat, he sat up. I held on, wrapping my legs around him like a piggy back ride.

"Now!" I screamed out.

He struggled to be upright. Squirming and flinging his body about as he stood and I wasn't letting go.

My arms were around his neck and he tried violently to get me off. My body felt every jolt and shake.

But I just…held on.

"Please, Vincent, please," I begged. "Let us help you."

He was a mad man, growling and shaking. He didn't care who I was. His hands reached back, grabbing for me. His nails digging into my skin. I could feel the sores as I held on to him. I don't know how long we struggled. But however long, it was enough for Martina to race forward at some point and jab him.

The moment the needle went into his body, Vincent screamed.

It didn't take long to take effect.

Clutching my son, I noticed everyone around him stepping back and waiting. Waiting for the medication to kick in.

Then it did.

His knees weakened and he tumbled down, bringing me with him to the ground.

Martina rushed over to him as Brian lifted me from my son.

"Are you alright?" Brian asked.

I nodded but didn't really register what was happening with me. I needed to know about Vincent. Was he alright? Alive?

He was.

My son was sedated.

It was time to get him the help he needed.

TWENTY-EIGHT

SUSTAINABLE

How I managed to do what I did to help stop my son, was a combination of things. A person never realizes that the life they had before being married, having children often gets lost in the life they gained.

I supposed a lot of why I was able to be so tough as an average built, often out of shape middle aged woman had to do with my past, my pre-Ted life, another had to do with my love for my son. Like any mother, I would go to extreme lengths to protect him. Some might say I was also aided by liquid courage, or Dutch courage as my mother used to call it, when she would drink before going to work on the streets.

That wore off and about the time I felt that post-wine headache hitting me, I felt every other ache in my body.

My shoulder was separated, of that I was sure. My back hurt from being twisted and the deep scratches on my arms burned.

That tranquilizer didn't last on Vincent. Maybe fifteen minutes. He woke up, was fine for a second, and then ripped the IV out of his arm.

In the midst of that, Martina hit him again knocking him out. We restrained him with belts and tape. It was nearly inhuman, but it was the only way we could keep him still. She couldn't give him any more tranquilizer or sedative for a couple more hours.

We hoped that before he had another episode that the medicine would kick in. But that was wishful thinking. He would need three days of a steady intravenous drip to start to heal what happened in his body and brain. That was if that could be done. There was a chance he had swelling on the brain, but there was no way without scans to know if swelling or sickness was causing the fits of rage.

Martina said, according to Perry, who seemed to know more about fungi infections, that the lesions would be a telltale sign of how he was doing.

I honestly couldn't see how they would ever heal. How my son would not be permanently scarred by what he endured, both physically and mentally.

Those lesions were so bad. About the size of a dime, they were virtually raw. Deep into the flesh. The skin surrounding each one was swollen. They looked like mini craters and the bloody mess inside was lava.

His left earlobe was gone along with some of his hair. He had a deep flesh sore that formed his top lip and like so many bodies that I had seen, the lesions hit his right eye. The lid was partially deteriorated.

In the world now, without plastic surgeons, he would never have an eye lid. His eye would never close, that alone had to be maddening. Burning, hurting, just thinking about what a simple blink does to keep the eye protected.

The lesions alone weren't what did the damage. Vincent did. The blood on his fingers and under his nails told me he picked at them, scratched them. They were already doing slow damage, he was just helping them along.

It was my assumption that some of that blood under his nails was mine, some Sonya's.

I cleaned my wounds and Martina gave me a dose of antibiotics, along with a topical to fight infection.

But she did so at least an hour after getting Vincent situated.

She was worried because we didn't know if the fungus was contagious. Sonya hadn't shown any symptoms and it was twenty-four hours.

Perry had dosed up Martina before they returned. It was not a waiting game. But it didn't matter to me. I was confident, if I got it, I would be cured because we'd catch it early.

At that point I was exhausted, sore and just didn't want to move. However, I had to radio my daughter. Even though Brian said he could reach her from the plane, I opted for the car. It just felt safe and private.

I needed to hear Avery's voice, and just talk.

She tried to hide her worry and said she and Al would pray for him and me.

"Focus all your prayers on your brother, baby," I told her. "He needs them. I'm fine."

"Mommy, if he can't handle the light, what happens in the morning?"

"We're going to move him into an office."

"Will you radio me again in the morning?"

"Of course," I said, then we told each other we loved each other, and ended the radio call.

I went back inside, checking on Vincent again.

I felt like a horrible mother because it pained me to sit by him, especially when he'd wake up every twenty minutes, thrash, scream, and yell that he hated us. It hurt my heart.

Still close to him, I found a spot just at the edge of the vending lounge and curled up on a golden vinyl chair.

At the three-hour mark, Vincent fell asleep. Perhaps the sedative took its toll. We kept the terminal dark; a small round battery light was on the table by where I sat.

"Here." Brian extended a bottle of water to me. "Do you need anything else? Maybe another drink?" He set a few little airline bottles on the table and a plastic glass.

"Um." I took the water. "Maybe in a little bit, thanks."

"I'm not gonna tell you to get some rest." He sat down in the chair across from me and coughed. "Your body will do that for you. But are you okay?" He coughed again.

"Me? Are you?"

He nodded. "Yeah, just a tickle in my throat. Nothing a drink won't help. Again, how are you?"

Mentally or physically."

"Both." He cracked open a little bottle and poured it in a glass, then took a sip.

"I just feel heavy. So brokenhearted right now. Like I'm wallowing in grief and my son is alive."

"Well, Lucy, it wasn't that long ago that you lost your husband. Those feelings resurface," he said. "Especially when faced with heart wrenching situations. Vincent is alive, yes, but he is so sick."

"You sound like you've been there with grief."

"No." He shook his head. "Not with grief. PTSD, had a lot of counseling for that. I know what triggered feelings can do."

"I wish I was stronger."

"Ha." He coughed then laughed. "You tackled that boy. No wait. You speared him. It's a wrestling term."

"I know what that is. Vincent loves professional wrestling."

"You must love it too," he said.

"Why do you say that?"

"Because of how you went after him."

I shook my head and took a drink of the water. "You know, sitting here I was thinking about how our lives before marriage, before kids, get lost. We forget what we were like, what we did. Well, maybe not forget, but try not to think about it."

"You were a fighter?" Brian asked.

I nodded.

"MMA?"

I laughed. "No." I laughed again. "Do I look like a professional MMA fighter?"

"I don't know, the way you took him down…"

"No, but thank you. I was life fighter. I went into the system when I was nine. My mom was a prostitute and overdosed with a client in a car."

"I'm sorry," he said softly.

"It's okay. It is what it is. I bounced around a lot. Foster home to group home, to foster home. I remember being so angry at her for dying. Not the life I had with her, I wasn't angry about that, because I never knew it was supposed to be different. I thought all moms left their kids with a microwave dinner and went to work. She was always nice to me and as I got older, I realized she wasn't in control of her problem or disease, whatever you want to call it."

"Did you age out?"

I shook my head. "No, I had a wonderful elderly couple take a chance on a scrappy fourteen-year-old. And they were the best thing to happen to me. The ended up adopting me, getting me therapy, making me pancakes. I mean like, from scratch."

"Wow, um, pancakes. That's a biggie."

I wagged my finger. "That was a bit sarcastic. That's okay; I'd never had anyone make me pancakes."

"So you stopped fighting then."

"A few scraps here and there. Nothing really physical, because I didn't have to fight to protect my food or what little belongings I had, and..." I added. "Pips, who was my adopted father would make me pay. Not the way you think, he didn't beat me. He would look at me and say, 'Lucy, I am very disappointed in you.' And that would do it."

"For what it's worth, I'm glad you got the pancakes and the parents you deserved." He lifted his glass in a cheers sort of way.

The corner of my mouth raised in a shocked smile.

"What?" he asked, seeing my expression.

"Ted said the exact same thing to me on our first date. Which I thought would be our last date, because, you know, who tells their life story to a total stranger?"

Brian widened his eyes.

"And I just told you my life story," I chuckled.

"We're not strangers when you bond under extreme circumstances. Ted, he sounds like he was a really good guy." He cleared his throat.

"He was. He really was. We met at a gas station when I was cursing out the pump because I thought it was broken. The truth was I just didn't know how to lock the handle so it just filled the tank continuously without me having to hold it in. I kept squeezing and letting go and getting more frustrated. Ted to the rescue. The rest is history. A sad history. But he gave me a great life and two kids." I bit my bottom lip, looking over at my son.

"He's going to get better," Brian said. "Trust me. I feel it."

"I do, too. I worry, but I know he will beat this. He has to. I can't lose him." I sighed heavily, then composed myself and looked back at Brian. "You know what? I will have one of those little bottles."

With a tightly closed mouth smile, Brian reached down, grabbed a little bottle, opened it and handed it to me.

TWENTY-NINE

UNDO

"Lucy."

Martina's voice sounded distant. Out of reach, as if coming from a mountain. I finally fell asleep and when I did it was deep. I didn't even know that she was calling my name to wake me, it was all part of a dream.

"Lucy."

Her voice was soft, without infliction, and when I finally felt the shake to my shoulder and registered how she sounded, my heart went into overdrive. I sat up, catching my breath. She stood above me.

"What is it? What's wrong?"

"Vincent. You need to come."

At that moment, all my hopes were dashed. She was going to show me that my son was either on his last breath or, worse, already gone.

I nodded to her and prepared myself mentally.

How long was I sleeping? The sun had started to rise and the terminal was getting light.

I followed her over to the corner where Vincent was being treated.

To my surprise and happiness, my son looked better. Yes, he still had the sores but they weren't as enflamed or as red.

"Fever down, his vitals are good," said Martina. "He's not reacting to the brighter room, but I don't want to take a chance, I want to move him to the other office."

"So, he's getting better?" I asked.

"I hope. We'll know more when he wakes. He's still sedated."

I inched my way to Vincent, taking his hand. He looked peaceful and that made me happy.

"We're on the right track," Martina said. "Today will be a big day with this. Twenty-four hours will tell a lot."

"This is amazing."

"It is. We can't do anything about the damage he did to himself, but the other sores look well on their way to healing."

"So, we move him."

Martina nodded. "Yes, to be sure the light doesn't irritate him. A precaution. I don't think it will."

"We're being safe."

"We are."

"Thank you," I said, reaching over and grabbing her hand. "Thank you so much." It was all I could say, my heart was full and so many words wanted to flow out. I couldn't believe it. It was a miracle. I took a nap and he took a change for the better.

"Thank Perry," Martina said. "It's all him."

"Oh, I will. Do you think he'll continue to get better?"

"I do."

Finally, something positive. I stood by my son while Martine went to wake Brian and PJ so they could move him. It was a break. A break in the hardship, the pain and there was hope.

I believed we were on the right path, that everything was going to be okay, until I heard Sonya cry out.

"Someone," she called in a panic. "Someone please! Please come here."

I walked from Vincent's bed around the corner to see her standing in the doorway of the ladies' room. She held her arm, cradling it close to her body.

"What is it?" I asked, hurrying to her. "Did you fall?"

She shook her head. "Please look at this and tell me it isn't what I think it is."

Slowly, Sonya extended her arm to me.

Her arms, like mine endured scratches at the hands of my son, her face as well.

"Please," she said. "Is that them?"

I looked down. Along the gashes were clearly four lesions forming. I lifted my eyes to her.

"They are, right?" she said.

I nodded. "I'm sorry." Whatever fungus Vincent had clearly was contagious by touch, probably in a similar manner to how ringworm spread. It wasn't just on her arms, I could see them starting near the scratches on her face.

I realized at that moment, if she had it, then more than likely, I did, too.

To beat your enemy, you had to know your enemy. The fungus infection was our enemy, unfortunately, we had no scientific equipment to study it.

The superstar bunker did. They had a medical division. Complete with a mini hospital. Brian reached out to them, and they stated they needed to figure out the best isolation method but wanted Sonya back to learn about it.

He informed them about Vincent's treatment. They didn't have that specific medicine on hand but they would send out security to look for it.

I told him they needed medicine for him. That tickle of a cough seemed to be turning into a full-blown cold. I made Brian promise me he'd drink a lot of water, not booze, and rest before he flew Sonya to Bunkerville.

Sonya wasn't excited to leave.

"I don't want to go," Sonya said. "Can't you just fix me here?" she asked Martina.

"I could start treatment, yes, but Sonya, if this thing is now spreading on its own without a delivery system, we need to know what we are up against. Your star powered bunker is the best way. You wanted to help, this is the way to do it."

"And we'll be in touch," I told her. "I promise we'll keep in touch."

"I caused this with Vincent," she said. "I don't want to leave him."

"I don't think you should," replied Martina.

I quickly turned to look at her, confused. "What?"

"So, you'll give me the treatment."

Martina shook her head. "I think Vincent should go. I think he should go with Sonya and get treatment there. I'll pack up what I have for him."

"No." I shook my head. "You're fine. I trust you. Why would we send him to Kentucky?"

"Because it's a millionaire's club bunker," Martina said. "You know damn well the doctors are top notch and if there are so many celebrities, I'll bet a dime to a dollar one of them is a plastic surgeon."

I chuckled. "You really think in an end of a world situation, celebrity or not, they are gonna have a plastic surgeon on hand?"

"Yes." Martina nodded adamantly.

"No."

Sonya interjected, "Yes. We have one of the best in the business in case, you know, anyone needs emergency work."

"Like what?" I asked.

Martina answered, "Vincent's eyelid. If there is a plastic surgeon there, even a more skilled surgeon than myself, we need to have his eyes looked at. Lucy, that bunker is a blessing right now. Take it."

"What am I supposed to do, just stick my son on a plane? A plane to God knows where the secret bunker?"

Martina's attention went to the sound of Brian coughing, then she looked at me. "No, I was hoping with how sick he is, that you would go along."

THIRTY

FLIGHT OUT

I needed to speak to Avery. I couldn't just get on a plane and fly off with Vincent without talking to her first, and Al of course.

Mr. Parson was there when I radioed, waiting impatiently for an update on Vincent.

He was happy to hear that he was improving.

"There's a bunker, Mr. Parson, a rich celebrity buy-in bunker. They have a medical center and specialists. Sonya has this fungal infection now and Martina thinks, even though Vincent is on his way to improvement, that he should go to the bunker."

"And the hold up on your end?"

"Is it fair? I mean all these people out there, infected, and Vincent is gonna get top notch treatment that others can't."

"Are you for real?" he asked. "Since when has the world been fair? It's always been like that. You think that since the world came to a halt that society is gonna be fair? You told Avery you ate beef Wellington, right?"

"Yes."

"Well, how is that fair when we're eating trout or others are eating crackers?"

"It was available to me," I defended.

"And so is that medical treatment."

"Martina wants me to go along because the pilot is sick."

"That should be your only hold up," Mr. Parson said. "Going with him or sending him off with you. Of course, the pilot being sick would scare me."

"Can I leave Avery? I mean, should I?"

"I think you need to talk to her. Hold on, she's outside, I'll get her."

My daughter was wise for her age. Mature for a teenager and I always believed that happened because of the terror attack and losing her father. She was thrust into an adult situation and no one really treated her like a child.

I was nervous about talking to her. Racked with guilt about wanting to leave her alone.

The radio hissed as she came on. "Hey, Mommy."

"Hey, Baby."

"How's Vincent?" she asked.

"He's making progress in a good way."

"I'm so glad to hear that. Is that bad?"

"Yeah, he is one sick pup," I told her. "And so much of it may not heal. But that's a conversation for another time."

"Why do you do that?"

"What?" I asked.

"Conversation for another time. You say that a lot. No offense, Mom. But the world is kinda messed up, if there's something that needs to be said, say it."

"Well, it's nothing like that. Vincent, just, the lesions on his face have done damage. It may be irreversible."

"Oh my God, my poor brother."

"Avery, honey, there is another reason I need to speak to you," I said, pausing before pressing the button on the microphone. "Sonya came from a special bunker. She came to find Vincent. I think I told you that. But, she's sick now. And in this bunker they have a medical area with doctors and I think a scientist. Sonya needs to go there so they can learn it and beat it so anyone else that gets sick won't die."

"That makes sense. Maybe we should send Vincent, too."

"Martina thinks we should."

"Mommy, if they are all famous celebrities, maybe they have someone that can fix the damage to Vincent's face."

"You sound like Martina. Baby, Vincent going isn't the problem. The pilot isn't well, like a cold or flu, and Martina wants to me to go with them to keep an eye on him."

"In a plane with a sick man?" she asked.

"Yes."

"That's scary."

"I know."

"What if he passes out?"

I closed my eyes. "Then I'll pull up."

"Pull up what?"

"The steering wheel or whatever, isn't that what they say in movies. Avery, the sick pilot isn't what worries me."

"What is?" she asked.

"Not getting back to you sooner."

"Mom," she said serious. "If this was me sick, Vincent would want you to go. I want you to get my brother better and bring him home. I want you to find out what the heck a fancy bunker is like."

Even though she couldn't see it, her words made me smile.

"I don't know how long I'll be."

"You won't be that long. I bet they have radios to stay in touch. They have to have the best stuff there."

"I bet they do," I said.

"Can I go back to our cabin though?" she asked. "I'm almost sixteen, I can do this. It's safe. Not that Al is bad, he's great, but I want to be in our home."

"I'll think about it."

"I hate when you say that. It's your way of not saying no."

"Avery, honestly, I will think about it."

We spoke a couple more minutes and she put Mr. Parson back on the radio.

"So you're gonna go to this fancy bunker?" he asked.

"I am. We'll leave today. It's only an hour flight."

"Will you radio when you arrive?"

"I will."

"And for what it's worth, a night here or there in her own bed isn't gonna hurt the girl. So, give it some serious thought. I'm not far, I can check on her."

"I get it. I'm just not comfortable with that," I said.

"I understand."

Mr. Parson was close, but he wasn't physically close enough for my comfort to leave my teenage daughter alone in the cabin. Maybe I would take his advice and have it start as a night here and there.

I didn't know how long I'd be gone. I trusted I would be safe in that superstar bunker.

They had security and probably more beef Wellington.

I sat in the car after ending the radio chat, thinking about Martina. Worried that she would be okay as well. I also felt horrible that they were about to undertake trying to save those sick in Cairo while I was jetting off.

"You have a second?" Brian's voice caused me to jump.

"Sure." I turned in the driver's seat to get out and saw him. "Whoa, Brian." I stepped out and shut the car door. "What's going on?" He looked pale and drawn and his eyes were slightly dark underneath. He was dragging and I could see it on him.

"Not feeling the best. Whatever this is. It really is hitting me now."

Instinctually, I reached up and touched his forehead.

He chuckled and coughed. "What are you doing?"

"Feeling for a fever. You have a temperature. You're really warm. Not concerning warm, but hovering around a hundred."

"Wow, is the mom in you equipped with a built-in hand thermometer?"

"No. Just experience."

"Because Martina just took my temperature. It's a hundred."

"Ha! Still. Fluids and ibuprofen."

"I promise, but first, we'll be packing to leave soon."

I shook my head. "I'll pack. You rest."

"Before that I want you to come to the plane."

"For what?"

"I'd like to take this chance to give you a quick flying lesson."

My eyes widened. "Are you that bad?"

"No." He shook his head. "But you never know especially since we have two people with that infection on the plane.

Vincent had outbursts and now Sonya is sick. I just want to be safer than sorry."

"Okay, let me grab something to take notes," I said.

He nodded and coughed.

I had a feeling that he wanted to give me the quick flying tips because he was far more concerned about his own health than he let on.

The empty mini airline bottles of booze that had been scattered all over the cockpit floor had been cleaned up. I had to admit that I didn't feel as if I had any more knowledge on how to fly a plane after our lesson than I did before.

"That was your crash course in being a pilot," Brian said. "No pun intended."

"Yes, it was. And I'm lost. I don't think I retained anything."

"You took notes." He pointed to the small notebook. "You'll be fine. If not, there's a help manual.'

"For real?"

"No, I'm joking." He smiled, coughed, and then brought his bottle to his lips.

"How are you feeling?"

"Better than them." He pointed back.

I glanced over my shoulder to the main cabin of the small craft.

Both Vincent and Sonya were in their reclined seats. Both covered with blankets. Vincent had an IV and extra restraints. Sonya was buckled in a little extra as well. Both of them were sedated.

While Vincent hadn't fully gained consciousness, we couldn't take a chance he was still out of control. And poor Sonya had started talking nonsense fifteen minutes before we were about to leave.

She was looking for her cat, and was showing signs of agitation over an ex-husband she swore took the expensive feline.

Martina didn't want to take any chances that either of them would be out of control five thousand feet above the ground.

She too gave me a crash course. Hers was on adding medicine to the IV and giving an injection, if need be to Sonya.

I bid farewell to Martina and PJ, and left them with a grateful embrace. I knew I'd speak to them soon, but I was still worried.

Getting Vincent and hitting him with the treatment was tough enough, and he was one, teenager, underweight boy. I couldn't imagine what they would go through trying to help dozens.

By the time we landed, they would be back in Cairo, coming up with their plan.

They stood to the side of the runway near the bunker waiting for us to take off.

Brian called out each control he touched as if going down a list. I sat next to him in the co-pilot seat.

"You ready?" he asked me.

"Yes. I am."

"We'll be there in an hour." He placed his hand on what looked like a gear shift. "Here we go."

We started to taxi down the runway. I sat back, drawing in a deep breath and double checking my seatbelt. I was always nervous when I flew, now it was in overdrive.

Deep down inside I knew we'd be fine. That nothing was going to happen in the hour flight. I just hoped our bunker destination was worth leaving my daughter behind again.

THIRTY-ONE

HOW THE OTHER HALF LIVES

The flight was fast and when I realized that Brian wasn't going to die on me or pass out, leaving me with the responsibility of landing the plane, I had a couple of those little booze bottles.

Vincent and Sonya remained sedated.

I talked Brian's ear off, keeping him awake. I didn't want him to doze off behind the wheel of the plane, if that was even a thing. More than likely, they're called controls.

He didn't seem to mind and even engaged in conversation when he wasn't radioing the bunker.

We talked about binging television shows, and if people back in the seventies had the means to binge watch shows, would they.

I firmly believed binge watching was an addiction not a bad one unless it interfered in relationships and work. I was a binge watcher. Ted was too. It was perfect. When he was home we spent hours not talking, just watching and eating. Then we'd discuss. The hardest part was keeping me away from looking up spoilers on my phone in the middle of the show.

But it was one thing I didn't really miss now because I only ever did it with Ted. Even when he was out of town, binge watching and the after-show discussions were always our thing.

Brian, on the other hand didn't think people in the past cared as much about sitting for hours.

It was a good debate.

When I learned he was one of four pilots in the bunker that got a free entry, I asked him what it was like.

"It's something you need to see for yourself. It's hard to describe. Different people live different ways. Are you a worker on a free pass, or an essential service person, which I'm considered, again on a free pass or are you a paying resident?"

"So, it's separated by classes. Like the Titanic."

"No," he chuckled. "I don't even think maintenance lives like that, it's more of a social stratification."

"I am so not familiar with that term."

"Social stratification is when different parties have different access to resources and stuff. Depending on who you are and what you do."

I nodded. "So, the maintenance man doesn't get beef Wellington."

Brian laughed and then coughed. "He probably does. More like he gets Jim Beam and not Pappy Van Winkles. Where I get Michter's."

"All bourbons?"

"Yeah," Brian replied.

"You're explaining class differences by who gets what bourbon?"

"Pretty much."

I found amusing that he did that. I didn't quite understand, until he told me the prices, pre-apocalypse of the whiskey.

"But, remember, I was there one night," he said. "Those folks need their bourbon, to them it's pretty rough being off the grid."

Off the grid? For real? Did he just say living in a luxury bunker was off the grid?

Ninety-five percent went off grid.

No phones. No internet, no television. We grew a lot of our food, hunted and fished. Bartered with our community neighbors.

I couldn't see what they considered roughing it or 'off the grid.' I know some hardcore people like Martina said I was a pampered person off the grid.

Maybe I was wrong. Maybe the bunker was this rust covered old silo with leaking pipes and rats.

Admittedly, I was slightly nervous and excited.

They were waiting for us and I knew by the six-figure Humvees that no one in that bunker, not even the lowest social strata-whatever, was roughing it.

Two black Humvees drove closer to meet us, they were large ones too, with four armed guards in hazmat suits and gasmasks.

They carried Sonya and Vincent out, taking care to not disturb his IV. They placed them in the front vehicle. It concerned me until Brian assured me we were all going to the same place.

We landed in an airport in the middle of nowhere. Just a wooden building with a flag on it. Brian and I got in the back of the second Humvee it was large and comfortable, they put up a dark privacy window between the front and back seats. I was ready to joke about putting a hood on our heads or covering our eyes when I realized the rear windows were too dark to see out of.

The moment Brian knew his flight was done and he sunk into the soft, leathery seats, he looked worse.

"Hey, we're gonna get you well soon enough," I told him.

"I know. I just need to close my eyes." He rested his head back.

"Don't die on me."

His eyes popped open. "What? No. I'm not dying." He coughed. "At least I hope not."

It didn't take long for him to fall asleep.

I checked my watch once we started to move.

We drove for a while, it was hard to know how fast because it was comfortable in there. The road was smooth, I knew that, smooth like a highway. I checked my watch again when I felt we left it for a secondary road. Forty minutes had passed and we traveled uphill, up a mountain, my popping ears told me that.

I also knew when we arrived.

I could hear the echoing sounds of the tires as if we were in a tunnel. And we slowed down.

One hour and ten minutes of driving.

Finally, we stopped.

I reached for the door handle and, of course, the child locks were on.

It took a minute for one of the guards to open the door.

I stepped out, as did Brian and I saw them putting Vincent and Sonya each on a rolling stretcher. Medical teams in protective wear pushed them forward toward a large metal door that opened automatically.

I tried to follow but the guard stopped me.

"That's my son. Where are you taking my son?" I charged.

"Lucy." Brian stepped to me. "He's fine. It's fine."

I took a deep breath and accepted his assurance. With being so focused on watching them take my son, I didn't look at my surroundings.

It looked like a warehouse, only with concrete floors and walls.

"Captain," a woman's voice sounded like it came from a speaker. "They will get the best medical care and testing."

What the heck? I thought. Where was the voice coming from? I didn't see a speaker until I moved farther away from the SUV. Then I saw a woman. She stood behind a slanted glass window and was a half floor above us. It looked like a control booth. Instantly she reminded me of a much less rough version of Martina. Same age, same build. Her hair was shorter and more auburn than gray.

"I promise you they will be fine and we will keep you updated. For the integrity of testing, we need to keep everyone separate."

"Where do we go?" I asked. "Do we stay here?"

"No," she replied. "Because this is a bunker, we do have a decontamination chamber you'll need to go through before we permit you access. We will decontaminate you, run some testing on you both, isolate you and..." She glanced down to a clipboard. "Lucy Carver for at least thirty-six hours. You understand, correct? You have been out there. Exposed."

I did understand, I really did. "What about my son. Will you keep me updated?"

"Absolutely," she replied. "I promise you will be comfortable and I will come to speak to you both once you get settled."

"He's sick." I pointed to Brian. "Can you have someone please check him?"

"I will do that myself. After decontamination." She waved her hand to the guards, and they escorted us toward the same door that they had taken Vincent and Sonya.

The woman didn't look threatening. I kept glancing her way as we were led out. She actually looked concerned as she watched us leave.

I was scared and hoped that the kindness she conveyed in her voice was genuine.

The decontamination process wasn't what I thought. When she mentioned bunker and decontamination chamber, I envisioned a small tile room where a steam comes down and mists you.

I couldn't have been more far off.

After undressing and turning over every item of clothing including my bra, I went through a three-shower process. Three different stalls, I walked from one to the other. Each smelled differently, the second one really medicinal and the last one almost fruity.

I wasn't scrubbed violently down like the movies. No one was with me. A red light above a door told me to stay put and when it turned green, I moved forward.

There was no powdery covering and I was given shampoo for my hair at the end.

A warm blast of air came at me from all angles. A blow dryer for my body.

A plain gray tee shirt, a pair of thin sweat pants waited for me, with slippers.

I realized when I saw the SH on them, it was Sonya's line of clothing. Comfy pants I couldn't afford, ever.

They really were comfortable.

After decontamination and getting dressed, I was taken to an area and placed inside. I heard the door engage and buzz. It wasn't like a prison or any group home from my past. It was warm and the lighting wasn't harsh.

I'd call it a rec room but it was more a living and dining area. A large room with a sofa, chairs, television on one end and a kitchen style table nearer to where I walked in.

At the far end of the room by the couch were two doors, and to my right, just before the sink and coffee station, was another door.

To my left was one of those observation windows.

"There's food in the mini fridge below the coffee bar. Next to the sink," the same woman's voice said. "Help yourself. Your room is the first door on the left. I'll be in to talk to you shortly. Answer any questions that I can."

"Where's Brian?"

"The captain is undergoing some tests."

"Do you have a name?"

"I'm sorry, I never told you. I'm Doctor Winslow, but please call me Phyllis. Relax, it won't be long."

I passively agreed but knew I wasn't going to be able to relax. I would when I knew about my son, Sonya and Brian.

Until then, I was going to look around.

The area where I was placed was near the decontamination bays, which led me to believe it was originally designed to be a fallout shelter, a place to go in case of nuclear war or something that caused radiation.

Pleasantly updated of course since the cold war. The self-serve coffee bar was nice. I could get anything from regular coffee to a latte. I opted for the latter.

The small fridge did have food: premade sandwiches, yogurts, desserts and beverages. When I saw the beer, even while my latte was being made, I immediately searched the cabinets for the whiskey. Not that I needed any, but I wanted to see what level those in isolation were considered.

I knew immediately when I saw the Jim Beam, we were the high-end guests.

That was okay. I could remember a time when Ted and I just got married that Jim Beam was out of our financial reach.

I wasn't hungry, not yet. With my latte, I went into the room they assigned to me.

Upon stepping in, I was surprised. It was a like a hotel room meets hospital. Yes, there were things in the walls, like oxygen and call buttons, things needed for patient care, but the room was really nice. The bed was beautifully made like the maid had just come in. The walls were painted with earthy tones and there was a huge window, with a small round table in front of it.

Of course, the window wasn't real. The remote control changed the view from wooded area to beach and night sky. Lots of options.

The privacy button closed a drape over it. Like every other window, I was willing to bet I would eventually see Phyllis on the other side.

I played with the settings on the remote and opted for a beach scene to enjoy my latte. I didn't need the forest, I saw that quite a bit. However, if I ended up there longer than a few days I was certain, I'd be longing for a view closest to the one I had at the cabin in Gideon.

The coffee wasn't bad, not for something that took less than two minutes to produce from a machine.

While sitting there, I kept thinking about Vincent, Sonya and Brian.

When bad things happened in the past, I don't know about other people, but my mind immediately started to fear the worst. I never assume the best.

I thought the worst of Brian's condition. I didn't know how he got so sick so fast.

At least an hour had gone by when I heard a voice, not Phyllis, over a speaker in my room.

"Miss Carver, your lunch is in the lift."

"I'm sorry, my lunch is in the what?"

No reply.

"Great." I tossed up my hands and began to look around my room. I looked near the virtual window because if they were bringing my lunch, that could be the way. But nothing there or on the remote.

Actually, the only thing in my room was the bathroom. I went to the main area and searched and I couldn't find the lift.

Then I just started to think smart. And headed to the hall by the secured door. Sure, enough, next to it was a small stainless steel door with a handle on the side. It looked a lot like a garbage chute. There was an indicator light above it. Tiny and green. I reached for the handle and immediately felt warmth.

When I opened it, sure enough there was a rectangular covered plate. Carefully, I removed it in case it was hot.

It was just warm. I took it to the table in the main room. I couldn't smell anything until I lifted the lid.

I chuckled amused at the food. It reminded me of pictures of airline food. Some strange looking pasta, broccoli, a mini loaf of bread and a sliver of pie.

It smelled wonderful and I was hungry. I finished it with a juice from the mini fridge and took the tray back to the lift.

When I returned, Phyllis was in the window of the main room.

"Miss Carver, if you'd like to go into your room we can talk."

"We can't talk here?"

"That's a different room for me. I have items to show you."

"Okay, and please, call me Lucy." I grabbed my juice and went into my room.

Just as I thought, my beach view window transformed and Phyllis was on the other side. She sat down close to the window and I sat at the table. Had it not been for the glass, it felt like we were in the same room.

"First," she said. "Your son is doing wonderfully. The lesions are healing and the scan shows minimal swelling on the brain. We're keeping him sedated until that swelling goes down. We expect a full recovery. I have a surgeon checking out his eyes tomorrow."

"Thank you."

"Sonya is in an early stage. Her brain is just starting to swell. She is confirmation that the fungus does spread through contact. We believe we will see results with her as well."

"This is really hopeful news."

Phyllis nodded.

"What about Brian. Does he have pneumonia?"

"Brian is a bit more complicated. This fungus is like anthrax in that it can be spread the same way. Subcutaneous, meaning through the skin, inhalation, and ingestion. Brian has the fungus in his lungs."

"Jesus. Is he going to be okay?" I asked.

"We hope. We're hitting him hard."

"And you said ingestion? People eat it?" I asked.

"Of course, as you know, we haven't seen anything here, but I am assuming since the spores are microscopic, they will be consumed. When that happens, that version is the worst. From what we learned, those fully exposed in the attack, were inhalation and subcutaneous, which is why they died. The ones that emerged, like Vincent, they touched something with the spores on. The spores become less active the longer they are exposed to air and not touching anything living."

"But a person is living. So, they can spread it. I can have it."

Again, she nodded. "That's why we're watching you."

"Wow." I sat back. "You're good. We've only been here a couple hours and you learned so much."

She smiled. "I wish." Then she lifted a tablet. "Right now, we are able to connect to the internet via a government server. The actual internet went down yesterday afternoon. Power in most places is now down. So, we are getting together all the information we can. We're in communication with others, with scientists and we are all sharing our knowledge. Until we can't."

"So, is it global?" I asked.

"We think just North America, the whole continent. We can't be sure about outside, but there's no reason to believe the attack happened overseas."

"That's scary. I mean, I know there's gonna be an economic impact, but we are sitting ducks."

"We are." Phyllis nodded. "I'm showing you the latest conversation with a scientist in Baltimore. He doesn't believe it is nature. That it was a weaponized spore from space."

I nearly choked. "Like aliens?"

"No." She laughed. "No. There are dangerous spores that lock on to satellites, most burn up in the atmosphere, unless it was harvested out there."

"So, it has to be someone with special technology?" I asked.

"Not really. They could have harvested it and it was stolen. No one knows. I don't think we'll ever know in our lifetime. We can speculate on what it was, how it hit us, but we need to focus on surviving. Curing those we can, and preparing for possible invasion. Not alien. I don't think that will come for some time. If there is a world left out there, they'll wait and make their way over to salvage what is left and take as their own. We would."

I pursed my lips and swallowed the lump in my throat. I lifted my juice and took a drink. "So until then we save people. Cure them?"

"We can't cure everyone that has it. There isn't enough medicine to do so. And from I am told, they aren't easy to handle. They're mad."

"They are. So, we help who we can catch."

"We do what we can."

"And then they'll just die," I said.

She paused before saying anything, then lowered the tablets. "Those like Brian and those who ingested it, will die without treatment. Those like Vincent, they will heal but not without limitations and disabilities."

"Such as?" I asked.

"The longer the brain remains hindered and swollen, the more permanent damage is done."

"Will they always have to be in the dark?"

Phyllis shook her head. "I don't know. Time will tell. We don't have enough data and again, we only theorize. But the theory being tossed around is, without medication, they will adapt. The skin will heal and they'll be out, day and night."

"Suffering from the madness?" I questioned.

"Yes. The best and most humane thing to happen would be for it to take their lives. But if it doesn't and they do adapt and change." she exhaled nervously. "We're in for a very scary world."

THIRTY-TWO

IN THE DAYS AHEAD

Three days.

I had been in the isolation area for three days when the door finally unlocked. I wasn't a prisoner by any means. I couldn't leave, but that was because they were being cautious. I never became infected with the fungus. They fed me well and I finished that bottle of Jim Beam. Phyllis kept twice daily radio calls to Avery through that little window. It was hard for Avery to not be able to speak to me properly, but I could hear her voice and that was what mattered.

The only thing I wish I had more details on were the health statuses of Vincent, Sonya and Brian. I was told they were doing well and making progress, but to be safe, they had to remain in an isolated medical ward until all signs of the fungus were gone.

I was given another batch of fresh clothes and truly was at a loss as to what was next when the door opened. Did I wander out, look around, or wait?

I walked to the recently unlocked door, staring at it as if it were some sort of trap. As if something would happen to me if I ventured through.

Then Phyliss appeared at the end of the hall. "I see you're ready to go."

"Except I don't know where."

"Follow me. I figured before we take you down, you would want to see your son and the others."

"I do, thank you very much." I picked up my walking pace to meet up with Phyliss. "Nice to see you not behind the glass. Thank you for being so kind."

"You're very welcome."

"You did not have to radio my daughter for me every day."

"I did," she said. "It was the thing to do for you. I am very happy you never got sick. That's hopeful for a lot of people."

"And I got scratched like Sonya."

"But you were given antibiotics," said Phyllis. "That may be the key. This way."

We walked a little further down the well-lit hall until we came to a door. "This is the observation lab. Much like on the other side. I can't have you near, Vincent, Sonya or Brian, but you can see them."

"Talk to them?"

"Yes, but there are some things you need to know." She opened the door. "On the positive side, the treatments work. Sonya got treatment early. She's doing outstanding. Vincent was very advanced and we stopped the Amphotericin B. It worked nicely. We also stopped the steady sedation and he appears to not have had any outbursts or agitation. We have another scan scheduled for this afternoon and I'm positive it will come back good."

"Sonya and Brian have they had outbursts?"

Phyllis shook her head. "Sonya has confusion. Brian never lost any of his faculties. But there are complications. Nothing deadly."

"What is it?"

"We think it has something to do with the infection. But, it appears, at this time, Vincent has lost his sight."

"My son is blind?" I asked, shocked. "He saw me the other day. Looked at me."

"I know. It could have been the treatment or it can temporary. We don't know, the scan will tell us. I just really feel this was part of the fungus in the body."

"He's alive," I said. "And getting well. That's what I'll focus on."

"Good. Vincent is resting on his own. So, if you don't get to speak to him now, you can come back."

We stepped further into the office or lab as she called it and she opened the wall to the window. When she did, I saw Vincent lying in bed. Already he looked better than the last time I saw him. His color had come back, some of the sores had started to heal. He no longer was in restraints, and I noticed there were bandages on his hands. "Why are his hands wrapped? Did something happen."

"When not restrained, Vincent picks at the sores. We're just being cautious."

"I see you're covering his eye."

"Yes, and we had a surgeon in. He wants to wait a couple days and do a skin graft to create an eyelid for him."

"When do you think I can take him home?"

Phillis looked at me curiously. "You're not staying?"

"Here at the bunker? I didn't pay for this and we have a place off the grid, away from all of this, that's unaffected."

"It's safer here. And Emanual said you are more than welcome to stay."

"I don't know who that is," I said.

"Emanual Lux. Billionaire."

"The tech genius. Wow, that is really awesome. But I can't leave my daughter behind to stay here."

"I know." Phyllis nodded. "We can have one of the pilots take you close to where you live. We can take Avery in too. Vincent needs to be here a few weeks."

"I can't possibly imagine living underground and seeing the world through a fake window."

"You don't have to stay underground. The compound is secure. Just sleep and eat under here."

I drew in my bottom lip, biting on it. "It's something to think about. But what are the chances I can go get my daughter here soon, bring her here and we wait for Vincent."

"I'll see what I can do."

"Thank you." I folded my arms close to my body and looked at Vincent. "Thank you so much for helping him. So, I don't suppose Brian will be well enough to fly me to Cairo."

"Brian is well. A residual cough, but he's not going to be able to fly you."

"Why?" I asked. "Is he in trouble for taking the plane?"

"No. No." She paused with a breath. "Brian is the reason I think it's the fungus causing the after effect. Brian lost his sight as well. It has to be a lingering effect of the treatment or disease, because what are the chances two of them are now blind?"

<><><><>

I felt totally devastated for Brian. So much so, I had to leave that medical bay without seeing him. I didn't know what to say, how to be encouraging. I could only imagine he was as broken about it as I felt for him.

His sight was everything.

Vincent was young. It was tragic what happened but he was young enough, resilient enough to learn to live with it.

After telling Phyllis that I wanted to step away and process it all, and that I needed to speak to Avery, she took me to a radio.

Avery was out working the garden and Al told me he'd make sure she was in when I called back.

The neurotic mother in me worried something was wrong with her. I had a feeling another shoe was going to drop.

After telling me she would look into getting me to Piedmont's small airfield, Phyllis led me to the floor where I'd be staying. The essential worker floor, the one just above the celebrities and rich. Pilots, doctors, some security.

My room wasn't ready and I was taken to Brian's room. It reminded me of a higher-end extended-stay suites, with a kitchenette, small living area and bedroom off that. It was extremely nice. The entire floor was beautiful.

All the room encircled a main luxury lobby with long tables to dine, and a recreation section.

I couldn't believe I was in a bunker. My initial thoughts were if this was the essential worker floor, how incredible was the rich people floor.

But Brian and Vincent's blindness wasn't all, and I learned that when Phyllis returned to tell me she had found a pilot that would take me to Piedmont and a security agent who would accompany us to Gideon in case of problems.

"Why Piedmont?" I asked. "I mean, I know it's closer but my car is in Cairo, along with Martina, Perry, PJ, the others. I'm pretty sure Martina wants to get home to Gideon."

"Lucy," Phyllis said softly. "We haven't heard from Martina or Perry in thirty-six hours."

"Is the radio down?"

She shrugged. "We were in constant communication. Last contact, she and PJ made it back to Cairo. They had enough treatment for a dozen people. It was daylight and they were getting ready to go out. We haven't heard back."

"You tried?"

"Yes," she replied. "We have tried every hour on the hour. Emanual has had people round the clock reaching out. We have tried every frequency. Found other people, but they weren't responding."

"Then the radios are down. You said there wasn't any power. That the electricity was down all over. Maybe that is it," I suggested. "She probably didn't take my car or else we'd here from her on that."

"You might be right."

"But you don't think so."

"I don't know what to think," she said. "Just fearful you know. That's why I suggested Piedmont."

"And that's why I think it's all the more reason to go to Cairo."

Perry and his son helped us out when we needed them, a simple lack of response wasn't good enough for me to leave them behind. And Martina was there for me and helped my child. I had to go, I had to find them. I couldn't abandon hope based on the fact that they didn't answer a radio call.

I had to believe everything was okay and there was a simple explanation.

I had to.

Bill. Just Bill. That was the pilot's name. I had a chance to meet him in the lobby area of the Essential Worker floor during our soup and sandwich lunch. He was sipping a one-olive martini and smelled like cigarette smoke. He had a gruff voice and was an older man, probably close to sixty-five. He was Emanual's personal pilot and had been since the tech billionaire was in designer diapers.

That's what Bill said, anyway.

He personally picked out Hanna as our one and only security detail.

"We don't need much more than her," Bill said. "She is brilliant in security and tough as nails."

He didn't present himself like a pilot that worked for one of the richest men in the world. He sounded like Pips, my adopted father, who spent his life working construction.

Bill told me his story. He had been working as a pilot for a budget airline, one that was going under. It was after his last flight; he was having a drink in the lounge when Emanual's father desperately came in looking for an available pilot. He had plane full of dignitaries and a pilot that was sick. Bill said 'what the hell' and that was all it took. He had been working for the Lux family ever since.

Hanna was the personal security for a senator. Bill personally watched her beat the piss out of a stalker slash attacker and struck up a friendship with her.

Hanna was the biggest woman I had ever met. Over six feet tall and muscular with super short hair. She didn't have a sense of humor. Not that I told any jokes, but I could tell by her demeanor she was a tough egg to crack.

I was grateful she was coming along.

After our crabcake sandwich lunch, I had enough courage to go see Brian and Sonya.

Vincent was still sleeping and after watching him for several minutes, I then moved to the next window for Sonya.

She was filing her nails and looked up brightly when she saw me.

"How are you feeling?" I asked.

"Better. Much better. I'm ready to get out of here. How's Vincent?"

"He's still not fully awake. But he will be. He had it pretty bad." I debated on telling her about Vincent's blindness, but opted against it. I didn't want her to worry that she too would lose her sight. "Brian is mending as well. I'm going to go see him next."

"Brian?" she asked.

"The pilot."

"I know who Brian is. Did he get the sores?"

"No, he got another variation. It hit his lungs. Again, he is getting on well, so I am told."

"Have you heard from Martina? I know they had medication in Cairo. Were they able to help anyone?"

"We don't know," I replied, shaking my head. "No one has had contact with them in nearly two whole days."

"Radios must be without power."

"That's what I think, too, but I'll find out. I have a pilot that is going to take me and a security woman to Cairo and we're going to go look for them before heading to the mountain to get Avery."

"What do you mean? Get Avery?" she asked.

"Bring her here."

"That is a great idea. It's safe here."

"It will only be until Vincent is better. Phyllis has a surgeon going to fix his eye and that will take a few weeks."

"Who knows?" Sonya shrugged. "Maybe you'll stay."

"I don't think so. As fancy as this place is, we have a great place in the mountains."

"I'd love to see it."

"Who knows? Maybe you'll change your mind about this place." I inhaled deeply. "Listen I'll check back later and visit you when I came to see Vincent. They're gonna let me know when he is up and talking. I don't think you'll be in isolation too long and that's a good thing."

"Tell Brian I am thinking about him."

"I will."

After she told me she was going back to paint her nails, I moved on. Seeing Brian was only a matter of walking a few feet to the next window.

I was nervous and ran through the things I could say to give him encouragement, in my mind. I prepared myself for a man angry and possibly depressed.

When I arrived at the window, he was sitting in a chair. His back slightly to me as he rocked a little back and forth. His hand was to his mouth, almost in a thinker position.

I pressed the button to speak to him. "Brian." I called his name again, to which I received no response and then noticed he was wearing earbuds.

Okay, I thought. *How do I get his attention?*

I noticed a small panel of light levers to my right. Three rows of four. I started moving the first row. Sliding up and down and they only controlled the observation room lights. The next row of lights were for his room. And as I flickered them again with no response, it hit me that, of course, he wasn't going to see them.

So, I waited a good ten minutes, feeling like a stalker. But he was listening away. Finally, after I gave him time. I watched him remove one of the earbuds and pull his earlobe as if they irritated him.

I jumped back and pressed the button. "Brian."

His head jerked up. "Lucy?"

"Yeah, it's me."

I watched him try to stand.

"Don't get up."

"I know you're not in the room."

"No. Not allowed yet. You look better."

"Do I?"

I cringed. "How...how, uh, is the cough?"

"Much better. I feel so much better."

"Good."

"I'm blind."

"I know. Vincent is too," I said.

"They didn't tell me that. Won't we be the pair? How is Sonya? Can she see?"

"Well enough to paint her nails."

"Good. I'm glad. They think it was the treatment," he said. "At least that's what the one doctor said."

"Phyllis?" I asked.

"No, some man. Can't remember his name."

"If it's the treatment maybe it's temporary."

"Maybe. How is Vincent handling it?" he asked.

"I don't know. He's been in and out, not fully aware yet. No more rage outbursts," I said. "How are you? I am really sorry."

"Don't be. It could be worse. I could be dead. I could have trouble breathing. I have had buddies lose limbs in the war, burned. This is something I will deal with."

"I'm glad to hear that," I said. "I was worried."

"Don't be. I'm on the mend."

"What kind of music are you listening to?" I asked.

"Oh, it's a book."

That confused me. "A book. Like an audiobook?"

"Yeah."

"Brian, you were rocking back and forth and bobbing your head...to a book?"

He chuckled. "It was getting me antsy. The author wouldn't get to the point and there's no pages to skip over."

"You skip pages?" I asked.

"Guilty. Especially if the author rambles or takes pages to describe a room setting. You see that a lot in authors that write apocalypse novels."

"Well," I said airily with a slight laugh. "Maybe you shouldn't have skipped ahead on those types of novels."

"They aren't training manuals," he laughed. "But nothing could have prepared us for this. Nothing. And the worst part. It's not over. I'm not talking about my health or the after effects, I mean the attack. It came on our soil."

"So, they been filling you in, as well?" I asked.

Brian nodded. "They have. Our attackers are like exterminators cleaning out pests and rodents before the next renter moves in. Once they feel the job is done, you can bet the new tenants aren't going to be far behind. We aren't ready. What makes it worse, and we can't fight them or defend ourselves. No one is left, and those of us who remain," he said. "Have to just let them walk on in."

THIRTY-THREE

FINALLY VINCENT

I was fine, emotionally, until the moment my son said to me, "Mom, don't go. Please don't leave."

We visited. Me on the other side of that window, Vincent finding his way to the sound of my voice. He told me he felt better and was hopeful that the blindness was temporary.

He remembered it all, all his episodes, and he was down in the dumps about it.

"I didn't see you guys as *you*," he said. "I just saw you as shadows, like monsters. Your voices were distorted and I just believed I was threatened and had to do whatever I could to survive. Crazy."

"It was the sickness."

"I know that now. But I could have seriously hurt you, or killed Sonya."

"But you didn't and you're getting better. Did the surgeon talk to you?"

Vincent shook his head. "No. Just Phyllis."

"Well, they're gonna do a skin graft to give you a new eyelid. You'll be here a few weeks."

"What about you?" he asked.

"Oh, I'm staying until you're fit to go back to Gideon." I paused. "You are going back to Gideon, right?"

"I want to. I want to go home. I don't know what I was thinking. I knew the danger. I spoke to Granddad."

"What? You did? When?"

"When I was on the bus."

"So, he's alive."

"He was. He yelled at me. Told me to get below, get someplace as air tight as I can. But I thought I'd be safe."

"Why didn't you tell us about it?"

"About the attacks?"

"Yes." I nodded. "Sonya told me that she told you."

"She did. She said she was going to the bunker and after the threat was over, I could come. But I didn't wait."

"Vince, answer the question. Why didn't you tell us?"

"You were safe and I knew if I told you that you would want to know how I knew and then you would take my phone and I wouldn't be able to go."

"You would have been fine at home."

"Do we know that?" he asked with edge.

"Uh, yeah, Vincent we do. I talk to your sister every day on the radio. Gideon is fine. It will be fine no matter what happens down here, or rather off the mountain. But now we need to find your grandfather. Did he say where he was going?"

"Yeah, and you don't have to look for him. He was going to his friend's restaurant and waiting it out in the fridge in the basement," Vincent replied. "Then he was coming up to Gideon."

"He's not there yet. But he could be delayed," I said. "I'll tell Mr. Parson when I see him that he may be arriving."

"Is Mr. Parson here?" he asked.

"No. I'm heading out tomorrow morning to get your sister and bring her back here."

"You're leaving?"

"I am."

Then helpless and sad, Vincent said those words, "Please don't leave."

Hearing them broke my heart.

"Vincent, I have to go get her."

"I'm scared, Mom."

"I know," I said. "But I will be back. A day or two tops. We have to stop at Cairo—"

"Cairo, why?'

"Because I need to check on Martina. She's not responding."

"Can't someone else go?" he asked. "Can't someone else check for Martina and get Avery?"

"Sure, someone else can. But do you think anyone is going to care as much as I will? No, Vince, I came after you and I will go after your sister."

I stayed and talked for a little more, happy that my son was fine. He didn't understand why I had to go and begged me to stay a little bit longer. I wanted to. But I needed to bring Avery to safety.

I had to get up early; Bill planned to leave as soon as the sun came up. I would speak to Phyllis about letting Sonya in to see Vincent and keep him company. I didn't understand why that couldn't be since they both had the same illness.

Then again, I wasn't the doctor.

I knew sleep would be difficult. I was nervous and excited, anxious to see my daughter and hold her in my arms. To have her with me, bring her back to the bunker and we would be a family unit again. Together.

The world was falling apart, but we would be together.

Unlike others in the bunker, I couldn't think about what would happen next, whether there'd be an invasion or more attacks. None of that mattered to me. I knew I could face it as long as my kids were safe.

In the bunker and in Gideon, we were. Everywhere in between was a danger zone.

THIRTY-FOUR

UNPREPARED

Several thin streams of smoke rose up, waving and dancing their way to the sky over Cairo. We saw them on our approach.

It wasn't a good sign. My heart sank to my stomach and I just wanted to vomit. The town wasn't big, a mere piece of land sandwiched in the folds of the Ohio and Mississippi rivers.

What was on fire? I didn't see any flames, just smoke.

"Should we keep going?" Bill asked.

Before I could answer, Hanna did. "No. We know there are survivors there. We stop. We help if we can. We can't just keep going."

"I'm gonna circle around," said Bill. "See if we can see anything down there before landing."

He tried. From a distance the smoke didn't look as bad or thick, but as Bill tried to circle, he had to pull around because it was deep.

Hanna asked. "What do you think the odds are that the infected started the fires to block the sun?"

"It isn't like they're brainless," I said. "It's a possibility. They just aren't thinking like you or me. According to Vincent, they see us as monsters."

"What if we are?" Bill asked.

"What?" I looked at him quickly. "What do you mean?"

"What if we're the monsters and they actually aren't. What if we don't see how we are and we were actually the one infected."

"Whoa," Hanna said. "Like a weird Twilight Zone episode."

"Exactly."

"Stop." I waved my hand. "You'll have me thinking about what is reality and what is not. It'll play this weird psychological thing to me. Like *The Matrix* did. I spent a week wondering if I my reality was real."

Bill laughed. "Okay I'll stop."

He made it like he was joking but a part of me wondered if he was truly serious.

We landed at the small airport and everything looked the same. My car was still there.

Bill secured the plane, just in case and we walked to the terminal.

It was a little messy but nothing we didn't do in the skirmish with Vincent. Martina had cleared out all of her things, nothing medical remained except the makeshift bed that Vincent had lay on. It was evident no one else had been there. They left.

"So, we know they headed back to town," I said.

"How?" Hanna asked. "Your car is there."

"Perry had a truck, and that's gone."

"So, now we head into town," Hanna stated. "We take your car."

I nodded. "It really isn't that far."

"I know you're not from here, but is there a place I can do recon before we go rolling in there unprepared?" she asked.

"I'm sure we can find somewhere."

Bill asked. "And how far of a drive is it to your mountain home?"

"About two hundred miles."

"How much gas do you have?" Bill asked.

"Oh, plenty enough to get there," I replied.

"And what about back?" he questioned. "We have to get back here for the plane. Power is out, the pumps won't work."

"Can't we siphon it or make a pump or something?"

Hanna shook her head. "Easier said than done. I mean, if we have to, we can. Bill, what are you thinking?"

"Does anyone up there have a means to get her down the mountain?"

"Mr. Parson has the Dodge," I answered. "I mean, he had gas as well, I think plenty to get her to Piedmont and him get back home."

Bill nodded. "When we go to your car. I need you to radio this Mr. Parson. See if he can get her to Piedmont. And if there's anyone else that wants to come. I can fit three more in the plane. If he can get her to Piedmont, then we scope the town. We look for the survivors. We fly to Piedmont."

"What about the survivors?" Hanna asked. "We can't just leave them."

"Take a couple with us to Piedmont and the others can take Lucy's car."

"Head them to Gideon," Hanna said. "It will be safe there."

"Exactly."

Safe.

The word 'safe' came up a lot. I wondered if an invasion from a foreign force had been a topic of conversation for everyone in the bunker before I arrived, because it seemed that was what they worried most about.

Yes, that was a concern, but our focus needed to be on what the threat was before us here and now. A foreign force didn't light Cairo on fire. Someone in the town did.

<><><><>

"Can you hear me okay?" With a hint of static, Hanna's voice came through the small speaker on the side of the four-by-four-inch square monitor she gave us. I supposed I would have heard her better if I used an earpiece, but Bill and I were both listening.

He pressed the 'talk' button. 'We hear you. Can you hear us?"

"Roger," she replied. "Headed into town now. Not sure how long the batteries will last, I'll put the cam on when I get closer."

We had pulled my car over just about a block and a half from what looked like the start of town. There was no one around and the smoke lingered not far ahead of us.

Hanna had come prepared, bringing that headset and camera with her. She was heavily armed as well, like Rambo, only a bit more extreme. An assault rifle, two hand guns, a huge knife strapped to her thigh and two grenades. I wasn't really sure what she planned on doing with those.

Bit extreme or not, she wasn't taking any chances.

I was glad.

Before we left the airport, I had spoken to Mr. Parson. He said he had enough gas to get Avery down the mountain and get back home himself.

I could hear it in his voice he was leery about us leaving and he asked three times if we were coming back. I assured him we were, and that I just didn't want to be away from my daughter any longer than needed.

Vincent needed to see his sister, as well.

Bill informed him that we would land at the Piedmont Municipal Airport just south of Piedmont and we would let him know when we were headed back to Cairo so Mr. Parson could venture down.

"Tell her not to bring a ton of stuff," I told Mr. Parson. "We won't be at the bunker long, just until Vincent's eyes are healed. And thank you."

I really was appreciative of everything he had done. I hoped I conveyed that enough. Just as I was appreciative for Bill and for Hanna.

It was a little hot in the car and I opened the door to let air in. I didn't want to venture away from the monitor, or move it since we were in range. I wasn't sure how those things worked. Plus, our car was our getaway, if need be, it was our only line of defense since Martina took the rifles.

As I balanced halfway in the hot car and out, I watched that screen and listened to the silence with bated breath wishing I had paid more attention to the town when I was in it.

It seemed like it took forever for her to reach the area not far ahead of us. Then again, she didn't walk straight down the main road.

"Should we go after her?" I asked.

"No, Hanna is fine. She's only been gone ten minutes," Bill said.

It wasn't long after Bill said that, when the static hissed on the radio and the screen on the monitor glitched and blinked trying to transmit a signal.

"I'm in," Hanna said. "It's not that dark, even with the smoke. So, if they are still ultraviolet sensitive I don't think they're out.

It was an action game, like a first-person shooter game. Hanna's point of view, the end of her rifle in the shot.

She moved slowly, looking left to right. Even though the images were small and in black and white, I could clearly see what she was describing.

"Doesn't look like all the store fronts are burned out. A few," she said. "The wine store and small grocer are fine. I'm looking for a pharmacy?" she asked.

"Yes," I answered. "It's a corner building, there's a side street that runs alongside of it. You'll see it. It's just before a blockade of cars."

Nearly biting my nails down to the quick, I watched. Smoke would dart in every once and a while.

"I see the blockade," Hanna announced. "I see a body."

She picked up her pace, the camera jostling as she did.

"Be careful," Bill told her.

"I'm fine." She arrived at the body, a man, his back turned toward her. "We have a male." Using her foot, she turned him over to his back.

The sores were all over his face, part of his mouth was missing and he was covered in blood.

Hanna crouched down lower to get a closer look. "Stab wound to the neck. He didn't die of the disease. I see another body."

She stood, causing my stomach to flop in a motion sickness way, then I grew worried.

"We have several bodies. Looks like some sort of fight or struggle went down."

"I can't…I can't look." I said to Bill and moved out of the car.

"Lucy," Bill replied. "I can't identify your friends."

"Another infected," Hanna said. "Okay this body is not. A female."

My jaw tensed and my heartbeat sped up.

"Is she one of yours, Lucy?" Hanna asked.

Scared to death and not wanting to, I looked. I hated to admit I sighed in relief that it wasn't Martina or anyone I recognized from the pharmacy.

"It looks like nine bodies," Hanna announced. "I'm not seeing any more. Let me check."

I stopped watching again until she said there were only two more not infected. While I didn't recognize the male of the remaining two, I did recognize the woman from the pharmacy.

"She was there," I said. "The last woman. She was in the pharmacy hiding with us."

"So, the people from the pharmacy were part of the fight," said Hanna. "Okay, I see the pharmacy. I'm going in."

I watched and seemingly walked with her as she stepped inside Perry's pharmacy. The shelves had been knocked over. It appeared as if there was a small fire near the door.

"If they're here hiding, where are they hiding?" Hanna asked.

"In the actual pharmacy part, there is a door, looks like a closet in the back."

"Roger that." Hanna walked, she made her way to the back. So many of the shelves were empty. "Looks like they've been looted." She paused showing a white shelf with a handprint. "We have blood. This shelf is antibiotics." She turned and stood before an empty case, the glass was broken. "Looks like they got the narcotics. I see the door. Wait."

The monitor went from the door to across the room. Two cots were set up, IV bags, still partially full hung on posts.

"They set up to help two people," Hanna said, walking closer to the cots. "There's blood on the sheet. The IV still has the shunt. Looks like they weren't having the treatment."

Bill glanced at me. "Guess that answers the question of if they tried."

"Headed back to the door now."

"It might be locked. More than likely it is."

Hanna reached for the handle and slowly turned it. "It's not." She pushed it open only slightly and called out. "Hanna Lawrence search and rescue. Don't shoot."

She waited a second and pushed the door opened wider, it was dark, and she put on her head lamp.

I gave her directions. "Go down that hallway, there will be a door to your right. That's where we stayed."

She didn't have to reach for the door for me to see it was ajar. Cautiously she pushed on it.

I don't know what I was expecting to see, but I knew what I was fearful of.

But when she stepped inside, she exposed nothing but an empty room. No boxes, no cots, blankets or sleeping bags. It was cleared out.

"Was this how the room was?" Hanna asked.

"No," I replied and took a deep breath. "Where did they go?"

THIRTY-FIVE

STRANGERS IN A FAR-OFF PLACE

Neither Bill nor myself were thinking straight.

When Hanna said she was on her way back, he asked if we should shut off the monitor. I told him I didn't see any reason to keep it on. She was on her way back and wasn't being stealthy. No need. It would take no more than a few minutes. I was still half outside the car and stepped fully out to get some air. I couldn't believe for nearly October how warm it was. Then again it was always so much hotter in the car.

I faced Bill, speaking to him as I had one arm rested on the door. "So do we want to radio Mr. Parson, tell him we're headed back to the airport?"

"That's probably a good idea." He reached for the radio. "Where did they go, Lucy? I don't think they're dead."

"I don't ether."

"They ran. Bugged out," Bill said. "Awfully fast, too."

"So, let's go over what we know," I told him. "Last we heard from Martina was not forty-eight hours ago. Fires are smoldering. There are bodies and a botched attempt to help two of them."

"Ever see *I am Legend*?" Bill asked.

"That's funny."

"What is?"

"Martina brought up *Omega Man.*"

"Based on the same book," Bill said. "But different execution. You remember how in the movie, Neville had the mate of the main vampire? How he was curing her."

"I do."

"And what happened?" Bill asked.

"They broke in to save her, they didn't want her cured."

"I think the same thing happened here. A rescue, a struggle, a fight and your friends were like, nope, no way we're out of here."

"Shit."

"What?" he asked.

"You're doing it to me again. Neville realized he was the monster."

Bill gave me a closed mouth smile, then the smile dropped. "Lucy," he said seriously as his head turned completely to look through the windshield.

I was getting ready to respond with a 'what' when I too, turned my head and saw them.

"Get in the car," Bill said.

There ahead of us on the road was a large group of people, all different shapes and sizes, organized into two rows. There were at least ten or fifteen in each row. I didn't have time to count.

Only for a split second did I wonder who they were, then I knew by the way they were dressed they had to be infected.

They had found a way to be out in the daylight.

Each of them wore heavy clothing. Long sleeves and long pants. Gloves covered their hands with tape around the wrist. They wore ski masks with sunglasses.

Clothed figures, hiding not only their identities, but their illness.

They weren't scared of us, not one bit. They were there to get us, attack.

They had bats and crowbars, hammers, axes, hatchets. Handheld weapons, no guns.

Once they had gathered in their formation, they just stood there, weapons in one hand, starting.

"Lucy, get in the car. Now!"

"Hanna."

"Get in the car!" Bill yelled.

I slid in and slammed the door, engaging the locks. The moment I reached for the ignition, the first row raced for us.

Bill fumbled to put the monitor back on. "Hanna, Hanna," he called out. "We're under attack. We're gonna have to pull back. There's at least…" Bill stopped when the first thump rang out. "Thirty. Hide."

They pummeled the car, throwing themselves on it. Front, back, roof. Everywhere. They banged with hands and the weapons they held.

I started the engine and reached for the gear shift just as a hammer came down to my windshield.

It was a man that did it, I could tell by his shape. He lay chest down on the hood of my car, hammer still in his hand and he used it to clear the shattered glass.

I threw the car into reverse and hit the gas. But the car barely moved.

Fifteen people on my car and behind it made backing up difficult.

I felt it in the vibration of the car and in my soul when I hit someone.

The bang and then the car bouncing as I rolled over the body.

I forced the wheel to the right, hoping the spin the car around when hammer man's hand shot through the broken window and grabbed for my face.

I couldn't see.

His fingers pressed hard to my jaw, squeezing it, trying to get a grip on me. I'm sure it hurt, but at that moment I couldn't think of the pain, I just needed to get us out of there.

I was staring at my own reflection in his glasses.

Bill reached over to try to free me. It was in that struggling moment, I realized I had stopped hitting the gas.

No. Drive. I told myself. Jerk the wheel and hit the gas, he'll fall off.

I did just that, turning the wheel hard at the same time my foot slammed to the pedal.

Hammer man released his grip on me and rolled across the hood. We were surrounded and my little wagon didn't have the power to plow through those who held on.

Crash.

Another window broke, then another.

I hit that gas as hard as I could, turning the wheel. A few let go but even more hung on.

One of them made his way into the car. His upper body hung half in the window of the back.

We were done. That was all I could think.

Try to pull away. Try to fight. It was mayhem. The car barely moved an inch and then it didn't move anymore. My wheels just spun.

They were on us. Four coming through the windshield. Reaching, swinging what weapon they could.

Boom.

The ground rumbled and the explosion was loud. The four on the hood jumped off and I saw through the corner of my eye that half the second row that stood in the distance, was gone.

Then I saw Hanna walking our way, raising her rifle.

"Go. Go," Bill said. "Go."

"We can't leave her," I said, then I heard firing shots.

Tat-tat-tat.

"Go!"

She had distracted them from my car enough that I could hit the gas, flying in reverse, losing all but the man that was half way in the backseat. Blood poured from his chest from broken glass, but he held on, trying to get in. It was time to turn around. I could still hear the gunfire. I turned the wheel again, swinging around the back end passenger side. Finally, he lifted up enough that Bill turned in his seat and kept hitting him until he let go.

Once he was off the car and rolling in the street, I stopped, pulled over to the side of the road, turned around and watched for Hanna.

She wasn't messing around. She was a woman on a mission, she didn't just spray fire, she aimed and landed her shots with precision as she moved forward.

Some of our attackers ran, some were defiant, going after Hanna as if their bats and sticks were a match for her rifle. Maybe with someone else, like me, they would have bested me. But Hanna moved like a video game character with perfect stance, her reactions were quick, never any panic moments.

I stepped from the car, eyes shifting from the man in the middle of the road to those who fell from her gunfire.

Hanna stopped, reloaded and waited.

After a minute, she bent down to a body and lifted off the hood. I couldn't see what she did, but she dropped the hood and kept walking our way.

"Thank you," I gushed. "Thank you so much."

She stopped then turned to the man in the road. He stumbled to a stand, then began to hobble. She didn't shoot him. Somehow to me that was more human.

Bill asked her, "Are you alright?"

"Yeah." She nodded. "These people aren't the enemy, they're just sick. But they're dangerous." She sighed out and shouldered her rifle. "Do you know if the people in the pharmacy hideout lived there?"

"They did not. They stayed there at night," I replied. "Just to be safe."

"When I walked through was it always that empty?"

I shook my head. "No, it was cleared out."

"We need to check town. Check for the truck your friend drove, all that. And then when we know it's clear and are confident they moved out, then we will go get your daughter. Is that okay?" Hanna said. "Because Lucy, I couldn't leave this place with a clear conscious without knowing."

"No, I understand. I truly do. Let's look," I told her.

"Can I drive?" she asked.

"Absolutely."

Then Hanna just walked to the car.

"She's not okay," said Bill, reaching out to me and stopping me. "She's not a killer. But I think a lot of this was residual anger."

"What do you mean?"

"Remember how I told you Hanna was security for a senator?"

I nodded.

"That senator was her husband. She wasn't a henchman, she ran logistics."

"You said you watched her beat up a stalker."

"Oh, yeah, I did," Bill replied. "She did. Election year, she came out and kicked the guy's ass. I was there because I just so happened to be at that rally. She was pretty bent about it, that's why I struck up the conversation. Joking to let me fly her away. We became social media friends and then in-person friends too."

"Okay..." I didn't know where he was going with it.

"Beating people up is not Hanna. She is tough. She is a great shot. But she is super focused right now. When Mr. Lux wanted security, I recommended Hanna. She said she wanted to make a difference in this world because she couldn't make a difference in her own."

"What does that mean?" I asked, then looked over when Hanna yelled and asked if we were coming.

"It means she couldn't save her own. She couldn't save her husband," Bill said. "He was killed and she wasn't able to save him."

"That's horrible."

"And you can relate," Bill said. "Her husband died at the Steubenville attack."

<><><><>

I saw Hanna in a different light after Bill told me about her husband. I wanted to bring it up but I thought doing so was tacky. I mean, how does one broach that subject? *Hey, I heard your husband died the same way as mine.* I knew her story, or some of it and that was what mattered.

She drove into town more confident than when she went in the first time. Maybe she knew no one was going to attack us.

Hanna asked if I knew where anyone lived when they weren't in the protective part of the pharmacy. The only home I knew of belonged to Perry and he lived on top of his pharmacy.

And that's where we went.

Clues that he lived, died, or left would be there.

It was a nice apartment. And I felt awful that it was the first thing that entered my mind when we stepped in. It was beautifully renovated and never would have expected something like it in such an old building. A lot of the things we assumed Perry would take were still there. Photographs, knickknacks, nothing personal was taken.

But there was no food and it appeared a lot of clothing was taken.

The truck was gone there were signs that pointed to them taking off. There were no bodies other than the ones found in the fight.

After we thoroughly checked out the apartment, Hanna spent forty minutes going through the streets, hollering out for anyone.

She'd yell that she was search and rescue.

No one replied.

Finally, she was satisfied that she did all she could and it was time to go.

Hanna gave a lot more effort than I would for strangers. But daylight was burning and if we wanted to get Avery and back to the bunker before nightfall, we had to leave.

Back to the airport.

Martina vanishing, that worried me, but I had a feeling she was fine. I really did. I believed she, PJ, Perry and others took off when things went bad and they did.

The infected caused an uprising and fought.

Some engaged, others just left.

Martina knew of a safe place for people…Gideon and without a shadow of a doubt, I believed that where she led them.

Hanna and Bill wanted to be sure. They didn't want to abandon anyone that could be hiding in fear. To me they went above and beyond.

I was impressed how unselfish they were. I couldn't be that way, I *wasn't* that way, because I was happy we were leaving.

I tried to help, not nearly as passionately as they did. Getting my daughter was my number one concern. And we were finally leaving to do just that.

THIRTY-SIX

THE BASE

Piedmont, MO

The airfield was just as empty as everything else was in Piedmont when I was there earlier. No signs of life, no cars. After landing, we taxied to the fueling station then Hanna and I walked toward the last hanger, we stayed in the open for Mr. Parson to see yet close enough to go inside if we had to.

There was a pickup truck there, no keys, but we really didn't look too hard.

It did have something Hanna found interesting. A map.

She had it spread on the hood of the truck, studying it like a weary traveler stranded on the highway.

I kept checking out the time, getting more antsy and worried about where my daughter was and was everything alight.

After looking toward the road a dozen times, I walked over to Hanna.

"We're not lost," I said.

She looked over at me with a dead pan expression. "Huh?"

"I was making a joke; you're looking at the map."

"Oh. Ha," she partially cracked a smile. "That was funny. Anyhow, where is Gideon Falls? I don't see it."

"Oh, you won't. It's not marked." I moved closer. "It's here." I pointed.

"There's no road."

"There is. Just not on the map. See this?" I showed her the one road. "This is the one that comes down to the highway. The road to Gideon Fall is about right here."

"So is Gideon between the road and the river?"

"No. It's like the song."

"What song?" She asked.

"Over the river and through the woods." I didn't get a reaction. "Anyhow, it's hidden."

"How far from the bridge—assume it's a bridge—is Gideon?"

'Two, three miles."

"Yeah, are you guys shit out of luck if something happens to that bridge," she said.

"Not really. We can walk. Mr. Parson did it once when he was younger. He said it took him two good days. It takes about thirty minutes to get from our community to this road. It doesn't lead straight to us."

"This, Lucy," she tapped the map, "is an excellent place. Honestly is a better place to be than the bunker if an invasion comes. You're cornered in the bunker, no matter how fancy. What is your cabin like?"

"More modern than everyone else's I suppose, thanks to Sonya. Can I…can I ask why you're asking so much about it? Not that I mind."

"I'm not sure what will happen when the attack comes."

"When?" I asked. "You're that sure it's coming?"

"For certain. Amber waves of grain. This country is prime real estate without you know, all us riff raff."

I chuckled. "That's an old term."

"I keep them alive for my mother. You are a very nice lady," Hanna said. "I really wish Vincent didn't come down. That you didn't have to see the horrors. My God, what a freaking gift those in Gideon got. Away from it all. Away, really, from what will come. I wish made that decision when Anderson died and I lost Baily."

"Your husband?" I asked. "And…"

"Son."

I gasped. "Oh my God, I didn't know you lost a child. I am so sorry."

"I was eight months pregnant."

I gasped again. "Wait. You ran out sick. You were in our group. I remember you."

"That tour was a blur, it was so hot and I just felt sick, like three minutes into it. I figured everyone was fascinated by Sonya and wouldn't notice if I ran out. I went out for air, threw up and when I turned to go back in. I saw these streaks coming down. There were four of them. Missiles. I tried to run, but," she paused. "I was thrown. The fall was too much for the baby. They tried to save him."

"I'm sorry." I grabbed her hand.

"You made the right choice in the mountain. I threw myself from behind the desk and into the field."

"For what it's worth, you are pretty kick-ass and I'm glad you're in the field with me," I replied. "And if you want, you are welcome to come back to Gideon Falls with us. My place is plenty big enough. You may need it." I waited for a response, and before I could get one, I heard the engine noise of that old Dodge.

I spun around to see the car approaching, stopping a distance from us in some attempt for dramatic effect.

The moment the Dodge stopped, the passenger door opened and Avery stepped out. I ran to her. Just as I extended my arm, I saw Martina exit from the rear passenger door.

I didn't stop the momentum of the embrace I was delivering to my daughter. I hugged her in gratefulness that she was fine and smelled like home. It was my intention to ask Martina about how she ended up in the car, but Hanna walked over.

"Is this the woman we were looking for?"

I broke from the embrace. "Yes. Yes, this is Martina."

"You looked for me?" Martina asked, sounding flattered. "Thank you."

"We looked for your whole group," Hanna replied.

"Our whole group didn't make it," Martina said. "Only nine of us. We fled when we couldn't fight them."

Mr. Parson stepped from the car. "She and the others were walking up the road when me, Avery and little Pete were coming down. I told her where we were headed, she wanted to come and see you."

"Little Pete took Perry, PJ and the others to Gideon," Martina explained.

Little Pete had been at Gideon Falls a long time, he wasn't a child, he was a full grown, middle-aged man that kept his childhood nickname.

"What happened?" I asked Martina.

"I don't know." Martina shrugged. "We had two of them, trying to cure them and the rest attacked. Just attacked us, violently, too. We hid until we could run. But they're covering themselves to be out during the day. I just wanted to see you before you headed back to the bunker. I'll fill you in on the rest by radio or when you get back." She paused. "You'll be back, right?"

I glanced at Hanna before replying, then pulled Avery close. "Yeah, I will be, without a doubt."

Martina nodded, not convinced.

I gave an awkward smile. "You don't think we will?"

"Lucy, you staying in that bunker will have nothing to do with the fancy food, high end neighbors, you staying in that bunker will have everything do with the fact that you are one crazy Mama Bear. You already proved you would go hell and high water for your kid."

"That's why we're going to the bunker while he gets the plastic surgery. Crazy Mama Bear?" I laughed. "Not really that bad?"

"That bad," Martina said. "Just brace yourself that is he is not coming back to Gideon."

"Oh my God," I gasped. "You think he's gonna die."

"What? No. I think that boy chased Sonya through a deadly biological weapon," Martina said. "He's not going anywhere."

While the mother inside of me was silently screaming my ridicule of her assessment, a tiny part of me knew she was right. My son, just a short time away from his eighteenth birthday, would make his own decision. As long as he was alive and well, Crazy Mama Bear or not, I would have to accept it.

I knew for sure I wasn't staying in the bunker.

Gideon Falls was home.

THIRTY-SEVEN

HOME

When I worked at the bank there was an auditor there named Felicia. She was not much older than me, but she was wise. She always said everyone in their life, at some point, goes full circle whether they want to or not. If they were lucky, it was a good full circle. Anytime a customer would 'go full circle', she'd point it out. Even if it was the long way around the block. Making it work, like the one customer born in Muncie, lived most of his adult life in New York, got rich, moved to St. Louis, but retired to Farmland, Indiana.

Born in a small town. Died in a small town. Full circle.

Felicia would never exit from a different door that she entered and would get upset at a book or a movie if she was unable to find a full circle connection.

Every good story had to go full circle.

The only reason I thought about Felicia was one of the surgeons in the bunker was named Felicia. Nothing like the one I knew, but the name made me think about her.

I wanted my story to go full circle. But what would that entail. Finding love, having a happy family. I wouldn't work at a bank again, not for a long time at least.

I thought about it a lot, because that was all I had to do in the bunker…think.

Think and listen to people talk about what is happening in the world above us.

I went topside a lot, it was fall and my favorite time of year. I hated the artificial windows and light.

Hanna was part of a scouting team that went out and checked the area every few days. Those who were inflicted by the haze were healing physically, but mentally they weren't recovering.

They were hostile whenever they encountered them, but they were surviving. A new breed of humans, created by the enemy. An enemy everyone patiently waited to arrive.

Hanna said she heard radio chatter from people on the coast that there ships in the distance. No one knew how true that was. There was no military that we knew of and none of the pilots wanted to chance flying out to see.

Brian would.

But he was far from being able to see.

While his sight was slowly coming back, he wouldn't fly for a long while, although he did discuss teaching me further.

I felt responsible for his illness, even though I knew I wasn't. He was out there for my son. If he wasn't chasing Vincent, he would have been fine. I made a vow to help him whether he liked it or not.

Avery fit in nicely with some other teenagers there, they had games and movies, and there was even a young filmmaker contest while we were there. She enjoyed herself, but deep down she couldn't wait to go home.

Vincent was well on his way to getting better. His sores had healed and as well as his mind, but he wasn't walking as well as he should have been.

Phyllis was wrong. She said a few weeks and that would have been correct if his eyelid was the only operation they were doing. But other than his missing lip, they wanted to fix his ear, fingers and whatever else he picked off his body while in a madman state.

Vincent's eyesight came back better than Brian's. It should have been a good thing, but really it just made things worse for him. Vincent could see not only what the sickness had done to him, but what he had done to himself as well.

Bottom line he was in for a year's worth of surgery and rehab.

His lip and eye he needed surgery on, but the other things were purely cosmetic and gave the doctors something to do with their time.

They were offering everyone to schedule enhancement treatments. I shuddered to think what they all would look like when they emerged from the bunker, puffy faces, small eyes and lantern chins.

We were at the bunker six weeks and I knew I couldn't stay there a year. I wanted to get back to Gideon Falls before the first snowfall covered the mountain road and made it impassable.

I spoke to Vincent.

Martina was right. He didn't use the surgery as an excuse, he was honest. He wasn't leaving Sonya. I didn't get it. They barely knew each other; she was so much older and from a different world. It bugged me.

But it was his choice. A choice I hated but one I vowed I would accept. Plus, she was good to him. It was never confirmed that there was a romance, just they both wanted to stay in the bunker, together.

It wasn't as if we wouldn't be in touch. We would be. In the way that the world was, we were just five hundred miles apart, we might as well have been oceans.

It broke my heart saying goodbye, but I pretended he was in college.

Avery was the driving force behind me being strong and walking away without too many tears.

Hanna and Brian both decided that Gideon Falls was the better choice for them too. I had plenty of room in the cabin.

I kept saying that I was glad they were coming somewhere safe, with a war on the way. I used the word 'war' and Hanna corrected me.

A war was when two sides fought. We had no army, maybe a navy out there somewhere, but no means of defense. In the eight weeks since the fog dropped and killed almost everyone, there had been no sightings of a government rising from the ashes to help us.

Nothing.

The only ones that rose from the ashes to fight were those who were sick. Perhaps they were the new soldiers.

What an irony it would be when the invaders actually came. The defenders of America were their own creations. Frankenstein versus his monsters.

We didn't fly back; we took a vehicle that would be good in the snow should we hit bad weather.

Avery made an off-hand comment about how we were going full circle if we were driving. Maybe she heard me talking about Felicia.

It was when Hanna commented, going back to Gideon wasn't full circle for any of us.

But we went full circle. A big circle.

Detouring out of the way on a two-day trip to Steubenville.

When last I was there, it was thriving, bustling with the prospect of the new plant. As we returned, it was dead.

The biomass plant still lay in a pile of rubble, a thin glaze of late fall snow was upon it. No one moved it or saved it. Old wreaths, homemade crosses and tattered pictures were at the entrance.

I thought of Ted and how he held such high dreams for that plant, how proud he was of it.

Dreams smashed.

Steubenville was the once a disadvantaged city post steel mill era on the brink of becoming a beacon again. It should have been known for new energy, but instead it was known for being the start of it all.

It was the beginning of a new life for all of us, and as sad at the stop in Steubenville made me feel, I was glad we went.

The detour would put a strain on the gas we had and it was time to head back and I felt confident my story had come full circle. Felicia would be proud.

I said goodbye once again to Ted. Trying not to think of the horrors of that day but more so of the joy he had given me.

We stayed on the highways as much as we could all the way to Piedmont. Highway driving was easier on gas and avoided the small town and cities where the maddened survivors had gathered. I was certain there were others like us out there. I hoped they were like us in staying put, staying safe from all the threats the world had to offer now.

The gas gave out and we puttered on fumes just before the small bridge and big hill to Gideon.

We shouldered our belongings for the last couple miles trek. I wasn't even sure the vehicle would have made it; the snow really started to fall.

Brian called the hike *interesting*. He was still unable to fully see, yet as he walked towards his new home, he felt the snow in a way he never did before.

We walked ahead of Hanna, because she insisted on moving the SUV. Drifting it down the road and off to the side.

She caught up to us, defending her decision in case anyone came. She wanted to throw them off. She spoke about taking out the bridge in the event of an invasion, shutting us off from any enemy.

I was happy she was planning ahead, Mr. Parson and Al would love that, but I didn't believe any invasion was coming.

Steubenville was the start of global terror attacks on energy sources. Whoever did it targeted everyone and everywhere. There was no reason to believe it was just the United States.

In my heart and mind, I believed the weapon just went out of control. If it went along with the theme of energy, to me, it was supposed to possibly drive home some sort warning about energy or global warming and it backfired.

A world that sought alternate energy because of overpopulation was thrown back to the dark ages with very little population.

Simplicity.

There were answers out there we would never get. Who did it, why they did it? I'd have to accept that and move forward, as we did on our walk to the community.

I held on to Brian and Avery held on to me. As we finally neared the area of the cabins, it was getting dark and the snow had reached my ankles.

The wetness seeped into my shoes and I could barely feel my feet. I thought about the cabin and how I'd immediately have to start a fire.

It would feel warm and comforting, just like the thought of going home.

Home.

Almost there.

We went to Gideon Falls to escape the world, to be safe from it all. And while the world changed around us, invasion or not, Gideon Falls would remain the same.

That's why we returned. It was warm, comforting, and safe.

It was home.

Jacqueline Druga is a native of Pittsburgh, PA. Her works include genres of all types but she favors post-apocalypse and apocalypse writing.

For updates on new releases you can find the author on:
Facebook: @jacquelinedruga
Twitter: @gojake
www.jacquelinedruga.com

www.ingramcontent.com/pod-product-compliance
Lightning Source LLC
LaVergne TN
LVHW091128080826
845145LV00008B/2078

* 9 7 8 1 8 3 9 1 9 5 0 3 7 *